I0555715

HOPELESSLY
HOOKED

BIG BAD DEEDS SERIES
ROSE SINCLAIR

ISBN: 978-1-7359375-5-7
Art Over Chaos Publishing
artoverchaos.com

CHAPTER ONE
— WARREN —

The ocean sang to me. The wind carried a voice even when there were no ships on the horizon. Despite not being near the shore, I heard waves softly crash as if they were outside the window as I held a ship in a bottle.

My plan for the afternoon had been to clean out the storage room of the last Queen's clutter. Yet I found myself almost frozen as I stared down at the model ship in my hands. The wooden model with sails at full mask showed off their dark color, making it unmistakably one of pirates.

The ship anchored my thoughts to the past as I pondered destiny. My life had gotten better upon coming to this town and continued to grow ever more peaceful after the Queen's death. And now because of a new King, I was able to build something for the future. A school by and for mages. The chance to heal more than broken bones, something deeper that might soothe souls. Capable of protecting its charges instead of stealing their childhoods.

The Queen had taken me from my parents before I even learned my real last name. I was given one in a royal court where magic was treated as either a bag of tricks or violence acted out on each other. Both for her cruel entertainment.

I hadn't ever been able to imagine that people *picked* what they did with their life until I crossed paths with a botanist. She was able to talk to plants, and only after I was lost outside a hedge maze was I truly found and given a home here in a quiet castle that was only ever visited when the Queen wanted solitude.

Under a moonless sky, the mage told me about my future here. She had foreseen that I'd fall for a man with a single ocean blue eye and forevermore go without a home on solid ground. It was easy to pretend I loved the fairytale romance she claimed when she was alive. Believing was the greatest way to show my gratitude for all the care she gave me.

But ever since, I've drowned out the call of the ocean because I *had* met the man I was destined to be with. There were no figures posed on the model ship, but I could almost see where he'd be standing. Men who lived at sea always looked like rough trade. But their captain had a duality around all those hard muscular edges with black curls flowing down to his shoulders.

My first brush with fate had been when his crew searched the town for a healer and brought me onto their docked ship. The Captain's hand was completely missing, and blood-soaked rags covered where the limb should have been. Given the extent of the injury, it was no surprise they wanted a mage instead of a regular doctor. This hadn't been the only time I've bore witness to the end result of a sharp cleave. But being alone in a room with a pirate captain while his crew waited outside blocking off any escape made my hands sweat.

"I can't reattach limbs." My words came out in a panic, weaker than they had been in years. Strangers in town often grew upset when I couldn't do the impossible after their trip to the castle. What would bloody pirates do?

The Captain looked at me with amusement in his

sharp, beautiful eyes marked by heterochromia. The mismatch made one brown and the other blue. "What's your name?" The voice was friendly despite the amount of pain he must have been holding back.

"Warren."

"Well, Warren," he said with a confident smile before his voice dropped to a near whisper that I instinctively leaned closer to hear. "My name is James, and I don't need you to return the hand. Heal me as I am."

My face flushed, and I realized how rare and precious that specific truth was. "Why would you tell me that?" I blurted out, my voice stronger now. "Don't you know the power a true name has with a mage?"

"Aye," James said, giving the vulnerability a beat. "But you seem more scared than I. No one fears a pirate with a commonplace name." He offered his wounded arm out as if to remind me he needed care. "If you'd please."

"Warren, are you feeling okay?" a stray child-like voice called.

Shaken from my memories, I blinked over to the young girl at the door away. "Yes, sorry. Cleaning these rooms out stirs up the past as well as dust."

Sophie smiled sweetly, before nodding towards my hands. "Neat ship. Are we getting rid of it?"

"Yes, please." I licked my lips and somewhat nervously gave her the bottled model of the *Jolly Roger*. She walked away taking the bottle with her, but I knew I'd see that ship again soon. It would be only a matter of days before

Captain Hook returned.

His reputation grew fiercer by the day. People believed he was so in love with the sea that it refused to take him down into its dark depths. A rubbish tale since it was *my* magic that protected him from all harm.

My intent had been to heal him like any other person in my care, but when I spoke his name and promised he'd feel no more pain, magic flowed wild and free. It curled around the contours in his name and stitched itself within his heart as the threads of fate hooked like a counterweight deep within me.

I might have well been a fish, given he seemed to be able to add or remove slack as if magic was on a reel. The *Jolly Roger* could travel the waves for months until he'd be all I could dream about. His words echoed in my mind for nights before he'd return under a new moon.

If Hook knew what he did to me, I'd cut our destinies apart. No matter the damage it caused. But ever since our deal, even lacking an explanation of any whys of magic, his behavior never hurt me. How could I worry about a deadly pirate when I feared the kind man within him? If only my fate was comforting. It stirred a panic over how hopelessly in love with him I might be if I ever let him truly near me. If he ever stayed on land…

CHAPTER TWO
— HOOK —

The sea was free of false pleasantries, politics, and boredom. My laugh bounced around with the thunder shaking the sky above. A soon-to-be-dead man stared at me with wide eyes that caught the crack of lightning glinting off the sword he ran me through with as he wondered why I was so amused.

"By the seas," the sailor prayed as he stumbled back against the very cargo we were in the midst of stealing.

I pulled the sword out of my sternum. Where there once might've been blood was now a glow of light that faded once the blade was pulled free of my skin. With the flick of my wrist, I welded it as my own weapon. "The cargo was worth attempting to kill for, but tell me... is it worth dying for?"

A chorus of weapons hit the deck, and another round of laughter rumbled through my chest. A one-man boarding party had been an impossible feat until I gave up the ability to live on land. Now I was unstoppable on the water.

My eyes scanned the terrorized crew before resting on the captain. "Do we have an agreement for your surrender?"

"Spare our lives," the fellow captain said, forgetting for

a moment that other things of value existed. "Take what you want."

"Gladly." I stepped over to a rope line that tied our two ships together, rippling the length to signal to my first mate. Smee was waiting with the rest of the boarding party, and within seconds, she and more pirates dropped in and started to liberate the offered cargo.

Smee paced in front of the sailors. "Anyone wishing for a new life may join us," she offered, expression stern solely because she hated that with a magical boost she didn't get to fight as much anymore. "The rest of you keep your heads down, and we will be out of your hair in no time. Any funny business, and my blade can finally have some action."

I returned to the ship first and was greeted by a man who always stayed on board. A quite colorful man given his two-toned striped pantaloons. When he asked for passage, he refused to give a real name—only a job title, knowing the value that truth held just like Warren had. We called him Piper since it was his instrument of choice. His blonde hair and habit of keeping even his fingernails clean never allowed him to look like the rest of the crew. Despite preferring land, he often joined our voyages since the money with us was consistent. In return, the angriest of the sea's moods would calm after a few notes of his music.

Piper currently stared at me with wide eyes. "Never saw magic like yours on land."

I grinned. "'Tis the whole point."

"The *whole* point would be telling me how," Piper insisted as he pushed off the railing and followed me along the deck.

With a deep laugh, I turned to him and crossed my arms over my unmarried chest. "Thought you said it was more poetic to claim I was born from the sea."

Piper conceded a quick nod. "Poetic indeed but not truthful."

"Dead men tell no tales; maybe that's when I'll tell you." As I stepped towards my cabin I heard a groan behind me.

A short time later, there was a knock as I studied a map I already had memorized. "Come in," I called towards the wooden door.

Smee stepped in with a pleased grin on her face. "Cargo is secured."

"Kill anyone?"

"Nay," she grinned and leaned back against the door, picturing something I wasn't privy to. "Tossed a man overboard. Sailors are so funny, always acting like they have to relearn swimming."

I smirked. Smee always loved a good splash and would usually toss her kills overboard for the added fun. "Glad you enjoyed yourself."

She pushed off the door, eyes falling to the map. "Piper wants us to head to land. I assume we are ignoring the request for another few nights."

"Indeed. No reason to waste a favorable moon."

"Aye, Captain."

In the silence after her departure, my eyes lost focus on the details as the answer to the mage's question slowly drowned out all other thoughts. There never used to be bad moons ruining my land legs for half of each month. A curse to most, but a mere inconvenience for a man as at home on the high seas as me.

In trade, there was only warmth now where physical

pain used to be. Being a pirate was the best life if one yearned to be free, but it wasn't an easy life. Or, at least, it hadn't been before Warren. His gift made me more brash and daring simply to get my blood pumping.

Oh, that darling, Warren. Loneliness rolled in as if on the tide. I attempted to wash it down with a swig of rum to no avail. He was empathy incarnate, and the yearning I felt towards him was the only pain my body was still capable of. My true nature was kept carefully hidden from him, lest he sees the vicious creature I could be and make me vulnerable once more.

Maybe I was too harsh the last time we met. Our rendezvous was always a private *non*-affair between the two of us. Last time, Warren spoke of a new King who showed up promising deeds and the types of dreams only land lovers had. *Maybe I was too dismissive.*

But what good ever came from men that traded soil that barely could be called their own? I groaned at the small dots of land and the coasts that marked the edge of the map as if they were personally responsible. Politics was for those who weren't free. If only Warren could be convinced to have a life at sea, the ship would never have to dock again.

In the middle of the night, I awoke to cannon fire. After quickly pulling on my jacket, I headed to the deck to see what was going on. The *Jolly Roger* was a fast ship. How'd anyone even get a jump on us? The flags of the other ship quickly held the answer with their red diamond shape.

A hiss of air escaped my lips. *The Queen's bloody fucking*

Cards. Give me an actual Navy compared to the random draw when it came to her old guards. After the queen died, they'd fled to the sea, becoming even more senseless and greedy without a purpose of serving her.

I'm not sure what the Queen once did with a guard so deeply akin to rabid animals that were now missing the cruel praise at the end of a leash. Piper was especially skittish of them. It took a long night of drinking to get him to reveal the symbolism in the Card's flags. Hearts had been tasked with fulfilling the Queen's whims and dark desires. Those who sailed under a diamond single-mindedly hoarded any type of wealth, ravenous beyond merit—now for themselves instead of the Queen.

I could handle a fight with these Cards without risking the crew. But cannonballs would rip through the ship before I could board, so I shouldn't waste any opportunity to deal with the smaller ship. Our ship was capable of ramming their boat to pieces if it came to it.

Below deck I found the gunners packing gunpowder and rushing to be ready to return fire. Visibility was low down here as I paced and took in a glimpse from each porthole. "Steady!" Once half of the cannons were ready, I gave the order to fire

Smee crouched below deck, eyes not even having time to adjust before she called out. "Captain, you gotta see this!"

I made my way back up, and a jolt from a direct hit caused me to lean into the stairs to catch myself. Maybe I'd destroy the ship out of principle just for attacking us.

A spyglass was handed over as I stood up and looked over at the other ship. The crew looked minimal, deck space replaced with cargo. I'd be surprised if they could even hold more if they could be successful here.

"Greedy bastards," Smee scoffed.

I stepped up to the wheel, and the man at the helm moved away to help elsewhere. The *Jolly Roger* was the larger ship, but it also wasn't operating with a skeleton crew, making it more nibble. "Let's finish them off."

There was a nervous mutter, and I glanced down in front of the wheel to find Piper hiding as he continued to mumble to himself. "Fuck, fuck, fuck."

My boisterous laugh did nothing for the mage's frayed nerves as I cranked the wheel around to position our ship around to their flank. "Not the best place to hide," I said, still grinning.

Piper's arms held tightly onto the bottom shaft of the wheel, and blessedly not in the way. "Think I'll stay near the unkillable pirate, thanks!"

I watched the ships come quickly closer to each other. "Aye, not the worst idea either."

"Heave, ho!" Smee yelled above everything, and our sailors pulled hard on cables to whip us around to build to a charging speed. Suited men started to jump off before our hulls even touched. But it was debatable if the choppy cold water was safer than the edges of the smaller ship as the middle started to crack apart.

The moment when the two ships intercepted seemed to drag on, but the *Jolly Roger* did not slow as we glided through, cutting the Cards' in half. Water was flooding in and smoothing us out on the other side as it slowly worked to sink the other ship.

"What now, Captain?" Smee asked. Bloodstained her shirt from where splintered wood had taken a small bite out of her side. Without a surgeon on board, I was just grateful it wasn't worse.

"Time out here doesn't matter. Let's head to land, heal the crew, and the damage to the ship."

She nodded firmly to me and then started to move around the ship shouting orders to the crew. Piper finally stood up, brushing off his outfit before giving me a nod and lifting his pipe. As his magical tune played, the wind billowed out the sails, speeding us towards land even faster.

"Land, ho!" The voice called down from his watch as my eyes held on the horizon line. A speck of dark color that slowly grew larger. Our navigator brought us closer to the shore as the other crew attended to the sails.

I'd seen this coastline more than most, but there was something off today. It took a moment to see smoke billowing up around the sharp spire the mages resided in.

When we docked, the area was cleared of the usual sailors and foot traffic. The air was thick with the scent of burnt vegetation. Curiously tugged at me as some of the crew ventured forth to investigate. Like a passing shadow, I quickly moved along towards a beach where we always found each other. Could Warren find me here if trapped behind the flames? Would he even choose me over helping others?

CHAPTER THREE
– HOOK –

The wide interrupted expanse of the ocean cresting along the shore was so marvelous and yet so different from riding the waves by ship. I couldn't help but find this overlap of the two worlds oddly intimate.

Warren picked the location after insisting on a neutral place away from the ship, and his daily life. It seemed we agreed on the same logic if not the same sentimentality. The problem was he wasn't here yet.

I took a seat on the soft ground and killed time by sifting sand through my hand like an hourglass. When the sun started to dip in the sky, I realized whatever pull usually brought Warren here wasn't enough today. Maybe the oddity I saw from the deck meant I had to go to him this time.

The Winter Castle was a gothic thing made of sharp spires and dark stones. Much of it was a large hall with a bell tower near the front. The building sat on top of a tall outcrop that looked over the city. What had changed was the land around it was now barren and burnt. There used to be evergreen hedges that blocked this area off from the rest of the town.

The fire wasn't actively burning as I approached, but there were still smoldering clumps of vegetation. A handful of people dotted the horizon against the lake, possibly protecting their freshwater source from whatever had happened here. It wasn't my business, so I continued up a long and narrow path up to the castle.

Under the arching doorway stood a young girl blocking the way inside. Behind her, leaning against a wall with his attention split, was a man who must have had ten years and hundred pounds on her. Over the girl's shoulders I spotted a series of tables with people at them. Their animated voices bounced around incoherently, but I didn't hear Warren's among them.

"Halt!" the girl ordered. "What's your name?"

I looked down at her. She wasn't a very useful guard; any sailor or dock worker would have the muscle to just lift her out of the way. "Is it needed?"

"Yes." There was no wiggle room in tone. She stared at the space between us, and sparks flared to life, crackling with a sizzle before blinking out.

I leaned back, surprised more than afraid of her show of magic. She could probably catch my coat on fire if I pushed my luck. *Did Warren have a pint-sized mage living here?* I smiled to myself and nodded towards the man nearby who was now only watching us. "Who is that?"

"I'm his back up," she said without a glance.

"Name's Captain Hook." I offered my hand out to shake, and she looked at the dirt there with a weak smile before opting to curtsy. "And who might you be?"

"I heard of you," she said, and I smirked. *As a pirate or from Warren?* "I'm Sophie, and I suppose you are already scheduled..."

Warren for sure. "No true name lore for you, young miss?"

"Maybe that isn't my real name."

13

The young girl was daring when pushed. I liked her. But she was also a poor liar and not quite skilled enough yet to pull off whatever twist of the tongue she wanted. The man behind her silently laughed to himself.

"Maybe." I nodded towards the stairs since her short height gave me ample room to see everyone on the first floor. "The healer? Is he still here?"

"Last I saw, he was in the attic."

I tipped my hat in thanks before heading up. Antiques, study models of the body, and sheets covering stone busts filled the castle's collection, serving as my only company until I found him at the end of it all.

Warren glanced up, lips parting. Then, he quickly pressed them together in a slight grimace. After a few steps closer, he seemed to believe I was actually in the room with him. "Why are you here?" His words barely lasted in the air before he went back to flipping through a book he'd been skimming.

"You missed our meet-up at the beach."

"You could have waited longer," he said, eyes not lifting this time. "Clearly, I'm busy."

I snorted, both to agree yet found the very idea amusing. With a quick movement, I drew a blade from my belt and ran it across my hand. Suddenly, the full weight of his attention was on me like a shark smelling blood. But I didn't need to look to know there wasn't an injury as I held my palm up. A faint glow lit up the air in front of my hand. All harm held back by magic. "It's weakening."

Warren swallowed roughly. Seemingly to push down an instinctual worry, he stepped over and took my hand. "Of course it is," he said roughly. He must've been saving the bedside manner for someone else. "We are under a quarter moon."

With a softness I came to equally expect, he moved my hand flat and hovered his over. My fingers flexed up on their own accord, wanting to touch even before the glow between us brightened, and magic shone as it repaired the skin.

"You know..." I said, letting my voice drop low and breathy. "You could leave me a few scars."

His gaze refused to catch mine as he pulled away. It only happened when Warren did magic, but I loved seeing his one eye swirl blue with magic pulling me in like a whirlpool. This close, it was easy to romanticize the man and believe that he could complete something within me. Or, at least, mirror me like we were a matching set.

"That's not how—" he started and then silently seemed to realize he had been about to go into magical teacher mode. Something he never actually did around me, despite being the head of this fledgling school. *Wish he would have.*

"And what story would this one have told?" Warren asked instead with a slight smile at least. "That the fearsome Capitan Hook is impatient?"

"Your protective hedge maze is gone," I said softly, knowing his smile would fade. His eyes caught mine like they were bound to. "I was growing worried about you."

He tugged his jacket firmly over his chest. "Don't be."

I stepped away, breaking free from the topic, and walked through the attic of this small dark castle. "So, this is where you live?"

Sunlight filtered in through the eaves, catching the specs of dust high up in the air. A floorboard creaked as I stepped over to an old rocking chair with a soft blanket pulled into the seat. Might have been a nice place if it had more fresh air.

"Yes."

Travel trunks sat piled on each other, not serving their true purpose. A couple were marked with snowflakes. Seasonal clothes, maybe, but I doubted they were his. Warren must have been here for years, but it didn't look much like a home.

My crew had far less private space on board, and yet they still personalized it. This was a prim and proper space designed for one royal and whoever else she could cram in a nearby closet space. The rest of the floor plan seemed jealously guarded between connected study rooms to match ever shifting moods. I didn't need to know the Queen to hear tales of her endless flares of temper.

I assumed the random disorganization started after the new King had offered lofty noble goals for revitalizing the space. Dusty boxes piled by windows were to be redistributed on the sparse bookshelves. "Starting to remind me of a ship. Except the books are the precious cargo to be divvied up."

After my self-guided mini-tour, I stepped close to Warren again. Waiting for... I didn't even know what. It was like an X had been painted on the floor next to him and simply felt like treasure could be found nearby.

A smirk spread across my face as Warren seemed to realize we were close. His gaze slowly dragged over my long coat making my pulse jump as if he was in true control of it. Every month we found ourselves in this game of chicken. I had long given up on him giving in and kissing me. Yet, it still remained a game I enjoyed playing.

He uttered a low warning that was distractingly sexy enough that I almost missed that the whisper held my first name within it.

A few beats of my heart later, Warren wrenched himself away. "I can't focus on buffing your spell when all I can think is the land here has no King and no protection."

I snickered without meaning to, and it was all the better that he pulled away first. "Your new king ran away already?"

"He's not–" Warren let out a steadying breath, likely to avoid his anger from showing and remembering I had no mind for the nuances of political games. "Yes, fine. My king is missing, and he burned down the only protection I've ever known on his way out."

"Tell me more about the hedge; make it a story."

The expression on his face seems torn. Then, he seemed to remember the safety that me being an outsider to his regular life offered. His tone was softer as his voice started spinning a tale. "Under the Queen's schooling, boys were made into bullies. My magic naturally heals. It wasn't what she wanted, and I ended up learning ...by healing myself."

"That's awful." The Queen was already dead and buried, but I'd happily dig her up just to serve justice myself.

"Yeah, when I was older she brought me here, and I got lost in the hedge maze. Felt like the plants were against me too. Then, I realized for the first time in forever that I was alone. And the silence was so peaceful. In the morning, the tower's bell rang, and I found my way back to the others."

I frowned, never liking a story that didn't end happily.

"But it worked out," Warren quickly added to reassure me. "Just being alone for a night in nature cleared my head. So, when the Queen ordered us to leave with her, I stood up for myself for the first time—told her I wouldn't go. I thought she might kill me, but she just looked down her nose and turned away."

"Never realized how important that maze was to you."

"Can't know things I don't tell anyone." Warren let out a bitter shaky laugh before continuing. "When the Wolf King came, claiming he wanted to turn this place into a college for mages, I felt like everything had come full circle. I thought we'd truly make the world a better place."

That second secret escaped him as his eyes prickled with sadness that shifted like harsh weather. His teeth gritted as he worked to keep speaking. "I'm so angry at him for destroying the hedge maze. Everyone demands help now, and there's no boundary to keep—" His jaw tightened down on the last words and locked the remaining thought behind his lips.

This level of candor wasn't unusual, but the hopelessness was new. "You don't feel safe," I said more than I asked. "My crew can stand guard. At least for a few days while you catch some sleep. Doesn't look like you've been sleeping well before this."

"You don't have to do that."

"Of course, I don't," I said and moved towards the door. His eyes followed me all the while. "But I'd like to if that's okay with you."

I glanced back as he looked down and wordlessly agreed.

"Then it's settled," I said, pausing to gauge if he'd change his mind. When his expression didn't shift, I pushed on. "The crew is at your service until I must return to the sea."

CHAPTER FOUR
— WARREN —

The night that the ocean didn't visit me in my dreams was the morning when I woke up to smoke. What had I been thinking to tell a pirate captain all of that? I hadn't been. That's the truth of it all. I stretched myself out too thin before everything changed, and now I was left with little willpower to resist his offer of help.

I never before invited Hook to stay in the castle. He couldn't have. There was a literal wall between me and anything that didn't truly need healings. Or, at least, there had been. It had been two nights since pirates became our guardians, and I found I didn't dream at all now. Maybe tonight I'd tell him to leave since I felt more rested than I had in years.

However, not everyone felt as comforted by their presence as I did. Sophie and her elder brother, Jonathan, were particularly wary towards them. Both grew up along the ocean and heard only the tales of merchants who had lost their cargo to pirate raids.

There was nothing I could do about it, so when I heard arguing downstairs, I assumed it was in that vein and made no rush to get ready.

Once I was closer, the ongoing argument made even less sense. It seemed Sophie and Smee were on the same side of a debate. "What's going on here?"

"This," Sophie started, censoring herself as Jonathan stood with his arms crossed, glaring at a new stranger by the door. "This man says his benefactor owns the castle and everything within it. Jonathan and I already told him the King gave you the deed to the property."

"And your part in this?" I asked Smee.

She didn't take her eye off the cloaked stranger. "Haven't been letting him in." Despite her rough, chipped tone, I smiled.

"Thank you. I'll handle it from here." I moved between the two groups and got my first real look at the person at our doorstep. My stomach lurched at the smell rising from him. A mixture of wet dirt and death despite his dedication to looking clean cut from his hair to pressed formal attire. I didn't know him, but I knew his type. "Did the Queen's family send you?"

"My name is Milo, and as I explained to your *comrades* here," he said with disdain, "these study halls contain rare magics that belong to the Hart family. I've been hired to bring—"

Milo's eyes shifted to look over my shoulder, and I found Hook coming down the hall with a determined pace.

"What are you doing here?" I asked the pirate. There was a book in one hand, and I was surprised that he seemed focused on de-escalation.

"Figured you favored the safety of your friends over some book this mage wanted."

There was a tingling warmth in my chest. The overwhelming weight of trying to fix everything *all by myself* shifted. If I had stayed in bed, this problem would have sorted itself out.

"He claims he's a summoner," Hook said bitterly.

"Ain't like any I know. Shall I kill him instead?"

"What? No." Maybe I should have asked *anything* besides what I did next. I studied Hook's face, and my wonder lasted only a second longer as I knew the answer before I even asked. "You'd kill for me?"

"Aye." Hook didn't seem to register my relief with his muscles coiled like a snake threatening to strike if provoked.

"Let me see the book." It was handed over with not more than a glance my way as four people tried to intimidate the stranger who thought he was better than all of them combined. I flipped through the book, finding spells and theories about summoning and necromancy. At least his story checked out. "He can have this."

I took half a step closer to hand it over to Milo before thinking better of it. There was something *off* about the magic within him, and I didn't want Hook or me near his magic. I gave the book to Smee, and she naturally knew to carry out the task.

"You have what you came for," Smee said, voice veiled with a violence. "Leave, now."

Pirates worked hard and played hard. I didn't think even half of them were drunk yet despite their rowdy volume that carried across the beach from the marketplace. A colorfully dressed piper played and sounded to have as much as the rest of them.

Gold flowed freely from the excess the pirates currently had. Drinks and food could only be consumed so fast, but by the way the merchants accepted their arrival, Hook's crew must be full of incredible tippers.

However, their captain remained next to me. Eyes on the water as if his soul was a compass that would always spin towards the ocean. In silence, I studied his face, unable to decide which side of his profile was better.

"Thank you for today," I said softly. Hadn't ever realized how much I might appreciate his help; only ever pictured him solving a fight by spilling blood. The fact that he thought of my wants first, and had been right, was a gift. Given the dangerous buzz I got when around him, knowing he'd throw down *for me,* it was a thrill. Even if it was a horrible thing to be so intrigued by.

"You're welcome," he said offhandedly, looking at me only briefly before standing up to venture towards the party.

"James, wait!" I hated how panicked I sounded. Desperate even.

He turned back looking hungry and protective in equal measure and silently waited for me to continue.

"Will you stay longer? Everyone at the college is still on edge."

Hook laughed to himself. His hand lifted to pantomime the words that followed, first down then in a tight circle. "Stay here, or stay around?"

I smiled despite myself. "Both?"

He'd go back to his ship in a matter of days when the moon was full. What harm was there in indulging fate just a little?

"Sure." He turned to me with an expression that made me feel like I was on the menu. "Now that you have me, whatever shall you do with me?"

Stars, maybe some distance was still needed. "Is sitting

22

together under the sun too boring of an ask?"

I thought Hook was about to lament my choice until he took his wide hat off and sat it on his lap, face turning up to the sun and breathing in the fresh ocean air. I closed my eyes to the calls of birds around us. As their songs grew louder, I knew they must be overhead.

"Don't see those much," Hook added.

To me, they were all seabirds. But they also must prefer to stay near the land. A gust of wind blew against my back, bringing in a chill from the water. "Afternoon wouldn't feel right without their calls." I glanced over at him, feeling silly but seemed unable to stop. "Are you like that with anything?"

Hook's eyes followed the birds, only dropping when they crossed over the crew. "If I missed a bird song, I'd just ask Piper to play it."

"Your new mage?" I asked. The musician hadn't come up to the castle, but I'd seen him around town before. I suspected he was a summoner too, and might call on him if the college ever had a rat problem I needed humanely solved.

"Can hardly call a man who doesn't like water *my* anything." Hook's tone was lively, but I couldn't share in the humor. His attention suddenly turned my way, and I felt caught until he spoke. "Would you care to go swimming?"

"No, thank you." A frown nearly gave away my feelings, and I kept my expression a neutral mask. "There are chores to be done this afternoon, and I don't want to get my clothes soaked beforehand."

He stood up and brushed the sand off. "Suit yourself."

With a longing I wanted to exorcize, I watched in silence as he walked into the water that eagerly lapped over his body as if excitedly welcoming him back. Even if I let myself fall for him, I didn't think a pirate would ever want someone like me for long. Someone whose world was shaken by the death of plants.

CHAPTER FIVE
— HOOK —

I stepped into Warren's room and found a far too narrow bed that didn't match the rest of the furniture. Wasn't even sure what this room was originally intended for with a door on each side; possibly a staging room that Warren had turned into his bedroom.

He was sleeping soundly with a hand hanging off the too-small mattress. I tapped my hook against the bed frame. The sound and vibration through the frame helped my efforts. "Time to wake up, darling."

Warren whined as he opened his eyes. For a moment, I thought I'd been too loud until he started blinking towards the light, then realized confusion was winning out. "Your little student almost woke you up three times already. I finally managed to convince her to stop by volunteering for the job myself."

As he sat up, the blanket he'd been covered with pooled at his waist, leaving a scarred chest bare. Now that was a bedtime story I wanted to hear.

"What time is it?" he asked.

"Early afternoon. I may have neglected to tell Sophie I'd only come to wake you after we finished all your morning duties."

Warren pulled his blanket up to cover his chest from

my gaze. "Your men did all my chores?"

"Wasn't difficult between us."

"It takes me all afternoon," Warren grumbled, lips pinching together afterward in a sorry show of gratitude.

"That's because there's like three of you permanently living here. I simply asked Jonathan for the list and divided it between all the crew. I like to keep them a little busy. You aren't lacking; you just lack labor."

His gaze set into a harsh squint. "Jonathan speaks to you now?"

Was Warren always this grumpy in the morning, or was he just suspicious? "Aye. It's also easy to convince men who grow up in port towns that you have something in common with them. Once you aren't a thieving outsider, you can quickly become friends."

Warren clutched the blanket tighter. "Well, now I don't know what to do with my day."

What a strange man. A puzzle box I wanted to get my hands all over and figure out the inner workings of until he opened up. "What did you do before? Before you started to burn the candle at both ends?" I glanced around the room, spotting his coat hanging on the corner of an armoire before noticing a paint-speckled bag hidden on the ground next to it. "Take the day off. Surely you have a hobby?"

"Course I do." Warren sighed, shaking his head a little before his eyes seemed to fully focus on me. "Fine, but I need another favor."

"Technically, you never asked for the first."

"Right." He stared down at his feet before leaning over the bed and shrugging on the shirt he found at foot of it. "This is weird, but you're being equally strange so... Could you not injure yourself today?"

"You know when harm befalls me?" Warren had been casual around the blood and bone when my hand was given a prosthetic. I had assumed that being a healer meant he was used to seeing injuries and left the heavy lifting to the magic. "The pain isn't transferred to you, is it?"

"No," he said instantly. "It's more like a stray thought that comes out of nowhere. It's just distracting, especially for time off."

"Do you mind if I drink?" I asked, raising the rum bottle he hadn't seemed to notice. His eyes followed the movement before shaking his head. "Would you like some?"

"No. Thank you,' Warren mumbled before stepping over to the supplies I saw, back turned away from me as he continued. "Stuff is poison for your body."

"Aye, that's why I make sure the crew always has a little work to focus on first." He didn't seem all that interested, so I dropped the topic as he lifted a bag that had been pinning blank canvas behind it. "You're certain you don't mind if I do?"

"It's your body." He shrugged carelessly. "Only wish you brought coffee instead."

I smiled to myself as he seemed to take my advice above time off, only pausing when he didn't even fully commit to looking over his shoulder to see I hadn't moved. I was curious to ask what else he could feel, but I worried he'd be scared off, so I simply took the nearest seat.

In an attempt not to just stare at him, I picked a book off a shelf and slowly flipped through it. Whether it was fiction or not, it was a compelling tale. When I looked up again, Warren was sitting on the ground behind a desk easel he sat on the floor along with him.

He leaned in to add more detail to a painting, not knowing how the image on the other side looked made my chest ache. As I stood, his eyes pulled to me like he'd been acutely aware of my position the whole time.

Warren's lips parted as if to object but didn't manage to say anything as I stepped closer and crouched down behind him. "What does it mean?"

"I don't follow," Warren said. "It's just you sitting."

"Aye, but this was made with a lot of feeling. I just can't tell which I'm meant to take away when I'm looking at it." The wet oil paint blended in a way that rendered a landscape of texture despite the limitations of this one room. There was something moving about the individualism that was captured, an awe in the mundane that almost rendered the scene heroic. "Almost romantic in its sadness."

Warren's hand quaked before he opted to put the brush down. "You seem to know your art styles."

I also knew the question that was about to form and aimed to change the subject. "What happened to make you so closed off?"

"You loathe politics. What do the details matter?"

"Fair enough." I stepped back over to my chair and resumed the sitting position from before. Or close enough as my eyes linger on Warren. He stared at his painting as if annoyed with it.

"What you've done is amazing given such low light."

Warren didn't look up, but he was facing me. I could still see the flicker of irritation that rippled over his expression.

"*Ah.* You don't want to be nice anymore." I was

certain I could see right through his flesh and bone to glimpse what was hidden underneath; a truth possibly trapped within his rib cage. His eyes locked with mine and seemed unable to look away. "That's why you should accept my efforts. It can be my turn. At least in regards to you."

"What?"

"Let me buy your art."

"No." Warren glanced back at the painting. "No way."

"There's not another matching this style in this whole place. Surely you must sell them."

"In the marketplace, *to strangers,* while I'm absent." His hand jetted towards me. "Not to people I know well."

"Fine." *I'll get a member of the crew to buy it later.*

"Fine?"

"If you don't wish me to buy one, I won't."

Warren stood up like it was the only high ground available and looked at me with disbelief. He sighed, a once hard gaze going unfocused even as he started to clean up. "I don't know what I've been thinking lately. The King made justice and change seem possible. Now he's missing, and..."

I didn't know where that thought was going so I couldn't prompt him to finish it. Instead, my vanity left me with an alternative. "Did you ever paint him?"

I needed to see his other paintings. He could get me to leave in an instant if he drew up a map of where to find them all. *Were there more by his hand down in the marketplace now?*

"No, he'd never stay still long enough."

This fact also pleased me. Do any of his other paintings

even have people? I stood once more, humming an acknowledgment to his words. As he lifted a cup of diluted paint water, I clinked my bottle against it. "Maybe you were looking for justice from the wrong man."

Warren struggled to speak, only softly uttering a syllable when he managed. *"James..."*

"I intend to be your justice." My tone is suddenly rougher than I usually allow around him. This time, I hoped he read the laced danger as in his favor and providing safety. My heart pounded as he looked up at me, chin tilting up as if to meet me a quarter of the way there.

But not quite enough. *Not yet.*

— WARREN —

By evening, I opted to make myself a fancier dinner. What else I was going to do, paint someone else and become utterly embarrassed? But it didn't seem to matter.

"Wait, what?" I asked, growing cold as Jonathan spoke. "Say that again?"

Jonathan leaned over the counter where I was cutting vegetables. "That musician is asking around town to find your paintings. It's the talk of the town given how much gold he is offering, so people even offered ones they already bought."

Fucking Hook. He never said he wouldn't get someone *else* to buy the paintings on his behalf. I hardly ever got the chance to paint, so there hadn't been many. Sometimes I'd do one if there was a bill that needed extra gold. What I had sold never left town. "I need to go; you can just have this."

"Warren," Jonathan said, and I was halfway to the door by the time he said another word. "Wait."

"Your duty is to your sister," I said, shaking my head at his unspoken offer, "not my personal problems."

By the time I got down to the shore, the dock's gentle sway lulled my anger. Then, like a fish given a second chance to fight for freedom, Hook stepped onto the deck with a smirk that brought back my annoyance at him.

"Warren, darling, to what do I owe the pleasure?" he asked from his ship. The piper seemed to be leaning against the railing with his back turned, but his head tilted to listen to us.

"You know exactly what you did. Using wordplay to lie to me?" I was so angry at myself that I thought he'd back off. Why had I believed his carefully selected words?

There was an angry haze in my mind until he offered his hand. "Come on. Best get you home before you turn green on the docks."

"You finally believe I get seasick?" How many times had I used that lie before? When the truth was it simply felt safer not to sail or be attached to anyone.

He smirked slightly as he moved onto the pier himself. I was equally as relieved as I was disappointed. The contradiction further weakened my stomach. A wave pushed my balance forward towards him as if it also cared one way or the other. Hook's arms steadied me, gently tilting my balance back to the center. The mood shifted as we were once again too close for my reason to hold out, and I was drawn closer still by the intense protective way he looked at me.

"I'm meant for dry land," I finally said.

"Just like those paintings were meant to be mine." Hook tilted his face down towards me, gaze fixed on my lips.

I fought myself and managed to step back since he didn't push. We walked down the dock, and I glanced back at the ship, feeling far enough away to at least speak in private.

"For a pirate, you're very respectful."

Hook laughed. "You think that because I'm a thief, I'd steal a kiss?"

"Just art."

"Aye, just art."

I just knew he'd be stubborn about this. "Can I have them back?"

"No. The trio I got today was rightfully paid for. What complaints do you have?"

"Fine," I said, biting the words down. "You aren't getting the one from today."

This only made Hook grin as we continued walking. "I adore that you think I haven't gotten someone to steal it already. Unless you were planning to keep that one for yourself?"

I flushed so quickly that I started to sweat.

"I want them." Hook's steps came to a stop as he turned to me. "And I want you. Is that so bad?"

"It's..." I searched for an excuse. We had moved far enough away that I couldn't say someone was watching us. There was even an embankment concealing us on one side. Everything was much harder to fight when we were alone. "What I'm really sick of is you having the upper hand today."

"What are you going to do about it?" There was a challenge in his words and in the tight set of his shoulders. But his posture was overall open and off-balanced, focusing on me.

I pushed him back towards the wall; the weight of muscle he had on me was meaningless at the moment. Hook's mouth met me halfway and not a sliver more. I paused as my lips barely brushed over his. *Fuck it.* Fighting this wasn't what I wanted.

My hands grabbed his collar and pulled him into a fierce kiss. His grip on my hip added a breathless game of tug of war. It took no further coaxing to elicit a growled moan from him as our lips remained locked together.

I broke the kiss, breath rough, but didn't wait for it to catch up. "Don't play word games with me, and don't underestimate me again."

"I never underestimated you." He tugged his clothes to right them and looked as devious as ever when his hook caught me under my belt and kept me from pulling away further. "But I won't. I only want to be a player in games you enjoy."

CHAPTER SIX
– HOOK –

I would possess that artist's heart as a crowning piece in my collection.

"Did you know the Wolf King had a boyfriend?" Warren volunteered as he stood in my cabin the following day.

I leaned back into my seat, determined to enjoy the sight of him onboard. "Did he now?" His every word felt like a tease after our kiss.

The mage nodded. "He came and went freely, which absolutely drove the King mad since he never knew for sure when his love would return."

"Maybe that's why he left." I kicked my boots up to my desk and tried to keep the conversation going. The very same event had caused the longest period I ever had around Warren, and I didn't want to risk any of it.

Warren leaned against the front of my desk, close enough I might be able to tap the tip of my toe against his leg. "After the King vanished, so did his lover. I'd like to think they went somewhere together."

"I adore happily ever afters."

Warren leaned forward to better look at the scrimshaw covered bone sitting on my desk. A whaler had carved a tale about a giant beast that made a six-man rowboat look tiny. In the distance was the larger ship too far away to offer any help.

"You wouldn't be like that, would you?" It was a question on his lips but hardly the one on his mind given how he was smiling at me.

"I always return here with the moon." The man I had bought the craving from claimed it was true, but I hadn't been there to confirm the truth. If Warren and I had a scene etched and inked, what would it say up to this point?

"Yeah. You do." Warren stepped over, and my legs swung down on instinct.

I was halfway out of my chair when our lips touched. I pushed forward to keep us standing.

Warren stepped back with a quick inhale as if remembering himself or some proper decorum. "I came here to discuss business."

"Have you?" I grinned. "Seems loose lips may sink this ship."

"Good," he dared. "Maybe then I'll be free of you and the *Jolly Roger*."

I tsked, trying not to take his cruelty personally. "That's not what you really want."

Warren's brow raised. "No?"

"No." His resistance evaporated as I maneuvered us around my cabin in a dance. His body gave way to trust before his resolve finally caught up to him and tensed up near my bed.

"Do you ever think of anything else?" Warren scolded without much conviction.

"Of course, I do," I grinned. Our old games were gone,

and I was eager to push on to see what could be had next. "Would you like to discuss trade routes or the weather?"

Warren scoffed and brushed past me. Magic buzzed across my skin, wanting to be closer again. I watched as he paced towards the door, then turned back. "The ask to parley was to discuss the long-term protection of the school. Maybe those on leave could—"

"Granted." The single word seemed to confuse him more than an essay would have.

"Thank you," he said with a frown.

"Are you ever happy, darling?"

His stern gaze fell away from me and over the new art displayed on the walls of my cabin. "Could you stop having people buy my painting on your behalf?"

"No," I said with a widening grin. "Does it upset you that I'm your biggest patron?"

"It's like a museum in here. Makes me feel..." Warren sighed, shoulders releasing the tension they were trying to hold onto. "Oddly at ease."

— WARREN —

Talk, secure the promise of safety, and return to the castle. That had been my plan. Yet, I couldn't get past the beach before pulling Hook against me. The more times I had to walk away from him, the harder it was becoming. I wanted something selfishly for myself, and this Captain was the only one who could give it to me. As if second nature, we made our way to our hidden cove.

My thoughts raced through overlapping beliefs regarding choice, destiny, and fate. Even the need to know that he was aching for me as well. My overthinking had brought us to a standstill. With his hands on my hips holding me flush to him, my hands hovered away as if not knowing what to do after first touching him.

"What are you waiting for this time?" Hook asked softly.

"I don't know."

He thankfully took that as an invitation to kiss me again. I moaned as his mouth claimed mine, soon gasping for him to take more. My hands snaked around his back and traced every inch they could reach.

I leaned back on my heels but refused to break the kiss, and Hook seemed to get my hint as we slowly fell back onto the sand. He kissed the corner of my mouth, then trailed along my jaw before dipping down over my neck. My breath gained an erratic edge as he went.

Thoughts lagged, and I broke out in a sweat as if Hook and I were doing something that needed actual endurance beyond him kissing down my neck. If I hadn't pulled away before, we'd be in the shade of his cabin rather than under the sun. "I'm so hot."

Hook pulled back, allowing the ocean breeze to flow between us. His face looked serious and concerned. It was a type of softness I never wanted to admit that he was capable of.

The magic in my heart cast a fast rhythm that I couldn't seem to settle. Usually, magic felt in my control, but near him, it sparkled to life with a heat that couldn't be contained. My hands dug into the sand, praying for some sort of hold before I melted. After a moment, I slipped on something smooth.

Hook held me against him, even though his focus moved off me. "You've made glass," he said, surprise lifting his usual cadence.

Unable to look away from his face, all I could do was ask what he meant. With a nod over to my hands, I was finally able to pull my gaze away and saw what magic did when ignored. Glass the size of my hand had formed from the mixture of magic, sand, and heat. "I've never done that before."

"Do you think your hands would burn me?"

I glanced back, stunned he'd even risk such a thing. The answer was on the tip of my tongue. I tried to bite the truth back with no success. "No, my magic seems to favor you."

He smiled softly and pulled me up on his lap, offering himself up as an anchor and, thankfully, still unaware that the magic within me did more than merely *prefer* him. It wanted to devour. To whisper the promise that once I had a taste of him, the gnawing desire would finally subside.

"Warren, darling?" he asked when I hadn't moved a muscle after our bodies had been pulled together even more suggestively than before. The kindness gave me the courage to put my hands on each side of his face and pull him back to my mouth.

With a slight shift of my legs, I straddled his hips and knew I was in trouble as my hands sank to his belt and hastily started to unbuckle.

"Are you going to regret this in the morning?" Hook asked, with a wide grin.

"Protecting my innocence?" I asked, pausing only to nip his ear.

"Never," he purred.

"Good," I mumbled before getting in another lick of the saltwater on his skin, expecting the taste but enjoying the pleased groan that followed. "You best not get back in that water until you finish me once and for all."

"Could never turn down booty," he joked. Then he squeezed my ass, and disarming me further by how willing he was to make himself a fool for me.

I rocked against him, cursing softly at our clothes and how good everything felt even with them still on. With a sudden urgency to make up for lost time, I pulled my shirt off first; then I tugged his up.

I told myself this was only chasing a release, to think of him like a pirate-shaped sex toy so it would keep things impersonal. But there was an uncomfortable pleasure as he slowed us down. For all of his teasing, claims of a good time, and eye fucking he still hadn't given me everything I wanted. *Yet.*

"We shouldn't—at least, not yet," he said softly against my mouth. "We don't have everything we need, and I don't want to hurt you."

"Why do you think you even could?" My voice sounded dangerous to my ears. A mad, delighted laugh came out of his mouth. "Think you should trust me with my own body. You already do with yours."

"Aye, that I have."

I pushed up, possessed with the sudden need to remove my pants as Hook watched, biting his lip and distractedly pulling off his remaining clothes. The tip of his hard length was slick enough with excitement that I could work with.

A hiss of pleasure was lost to the sound of the waves crashing as I slowly lowered myself onto him. For the first few moments, it took active focus on the mechanics so magic could flow and make my bodily desires possible on demand.

Hook leaned his head back, clearly enjoying himself without any extra thoughts on his end. "You're not supposed to be able to do that."

"I know what bodies need." I grinned, enjoying being the exception. Soon, I relaxed enough to open up further and fucked myself down on him with no more thought than it took my heart to beat. "And know mine intimately."

I shivered as something cold touched my thigh and found his hands in my lap before one greedily started to stroke my cock. Soon, we became lost to the rhythm of our own making. I moaned deeper as Hook sucked on my pulse point.

"Seasick," he mocked. "You move like the ocean."

There was a hitch in my hips, the 'waves' settled into a calm. "I don't know what that means."

"Let me take you out on the ship," Hook said, voice filled with heat, "and I'll show you."

"You're lucky I'm letting you *take* me on land," I grinned. "Don't push your luck, pirate."

Hook mumbled a pleased little cuss. His name had always been a thing of power in my mouth, and even withholding it seemed to have him spellbound. He thrust up, setting his own pace that drove me wild.

I tried to kiss, but my soft gasps kept stealing my focus as the easy glide of his hand signaled the finish line was within reach. I didn't know how he lasted, but I cried out as pleasure took hold of me. "Ah—*James!*"

There was something hot and dangerous, but no added magic. *Just us.* And all the vulnerability I'd been withholding releasing. A complete free fall of feelings until he spoke.

"Ride it out; I got you."

I felt as if floating, like the comforting current within my bones could never drown me. To blissed out to even register what I was doing until his voice brought me back again.

"You need to stop twitching like that," Hook warned. His tone was crass, and exactly what you'd expect of a fearsome pirate.

We were already marked by fate. What was a little more from a man who couldn't hurt me? I only made it another game between us—one I refused to lose or back down from now.

"Like this?" I teased and tensed around him.

"*Mmm...* yeah." Hook's hand squeezed my hip and guided our bodies as one until he couldn't take anymore and lost control of himself within me. I might have started to feel like the toy if he didn't groan my name like a wish coming true as he came.

He couldn't lift me with one hand, so I carefully moved up enough to separate us and sat back down next to him. I realized that I'd been a fool to think he'd be more spent. The slight effort sapped the last of my strength.

He ran a hand through my hair, and my heavy eyelids closed as I leaned into his shoulder, wanting nothing more than to just stay next to him on the beach.

"We should get in the ocean," Hook said as he stood. "Rinse off."

Lazily, I looked to where he was more near my feet. "If you could pick me up, you could probably kidnap me right now."

"Don't tempt me." He laughed as I started to push myself up. "Here."

I paused to find a hook offered to help me up. My fingers curiously reached up to curl around the metal. With a confident tug, he pulled me up to my feet so fast that I lost my breath.

Fuck, he was strong.

Hook just raised a brow. "You okay there?"

I just nodded as he stepped over to the water, and the call of magic softly sang to me to follow. Deep trouble was ahead for me if I already was yearning to stay close.

CHAPTER SEVEN
— HOOK —

I think artists are incapable of making anything besides love. Even when they were hard, brushing, or brash. Everything they did was an act of devoted feeling. Joy, pleasure, anything and everything that words weren't wholly shaped for.

The water effortlessly washed us clean, and we silently held each other. I knew much about the hearts of men at sea but little of artists. Always found them surprisingly skittish for the boldness they possessed.

Warren picked a great beach, not a soul interrupted or even came within eyesight. I wasn't sure how much time it bought us to stay like that, but a moment more was worth it. He looked fully relaxed for the first time since I'd known him.

"I've wanted to do that for a long time," I said.

Warren smiled down into the water. "Hadn't noticed," he teased.

We made our way back to our clothes, which proved harder to get into than out of given our dipping wet bodies. I had the advantage of practice and finished first. I ventured back to where we were before and dug out the glass he made. With the tip of my hook, I flipped over the flat surface created by his magical touch. The fulgurite

Warren made mimicked the path of lightning as it dispersed into the ground, making it look almost like bleached coral. But, unlike the natural counterpart, Warren's creation was clear like glass. My other hand reached down to carefully pick it up, and I was stunned into silence that something like this was even possible.

"What are you doing?" he asked.

I glanced up to see Warren's brow wrinkle. "Keeping this as a souvenir."

He swallowed roughly, not meeting my gaze as he stared at the glass sculpture. "Don't do that."

"Why not? I'm not going to tell anyone how it was made," I said with a gentle laugh. "That's for me to grin at every time I see it."

Warren paled, embarrassment rendering him speechless. He truly did not appreciate all the things he was capable of. My smile stayed soft and never caved into a darkly pleased feeling inside my chest. What a darling little thing he was to be so brash and yet be flustered over his magic slipping beyond his control for a second and making something so beautiful.

"Do you always take what you want?" His tone gained a harsh edge, causing a laugh to escape me considering everything.

"Don't you?"

"I never do," Warren confessed in a single breath. "You're the oddity."

"I'd say it's a good look on you, but I think you'd look wonderful doing anything." My fingers snaked around the glass sculpture, determined to take it back to my cabin.

As if knowing I wouldn't be deterred, Warren finally smiled. "Thank you," he said, giving a small pause. "You can't be on land after today."

There was no extra sadness in the words. An observation of mere fact as my eyes lifted to the moon keeping us company even in the daylight. "Not for a bit, no. We won't set sail until we work out the details for your college."

"Right." A frown followed, and I wondered if he had forgotten about it for a moment. His hands folded together behind his back. "We can discuss it more soon."

— WARREN —

Having sex wasn't a mistake; it was letting him hold me afterward as the waves continued to push us towards each other. Could I live with having a relationship with a man who couldn't be on land half the month? Especially when that annoying quirk was *my* fault.

Even if I could, what if we broke up and my magic soured on him? I didn't want him hurt. Didn't want his crew to be harmed because he thought he was invincible only to find out he wasn't amid battle.

My head refused to focus on any of my other work until I headed towards the decks the following day. There was a crew on the deck making preparations, but they didn't appear to be in any hurry. I walked aboard and glanced at other pirates as if they'd chew me out for being here. The most I got was a friendly nod as one made eye contact.

With a deep breath, I headed towards the Captain's cabin and tapped the back of my knuckles against the door, waiting for a voice inside that told me to step inside.

Hook glanced up from whatever he was doing with a bold smile that fired a deep want in my core. Control of my thoughts slipped whenever he looked at me, and I barely could stand it.

My eyes glanced at the maps over his desk. I had no idea what he was planning, but I didn't think it mattered all that much. "You know, I could accidentally kill you if I broke your heart."

His hook lifted to carefully scratch at his temple. "Then don't break it?"

"It's not that simple." *Why did I start the conversation this way?* I didn't even want to talk about this. Let alone sound so antagonistic about it. I needed to focus on the future, the college, and the mages that would need my help. Not whatever was between us.

"Clearly." His words were hushed and maddeningly careful as if trying to be quiet enough to listen in on my thoughts and hear what I wasn't saying. But there was also an annoyance shown in how his muscles tensed up.

"Why are you getting upset with me?"

His arms lifted, giving up in his attempt to figure me out. "You can let go of your spell over me at any time."

I wasn't sure I actually could. The pull of fate was what had scared me since the day I laid eyes on him. But admitting that to him meant giving up the assumed level of control I had over the spell.

Hook stared. Neither of us spoke or moved for a long moment until he was the first. "You're obviously getting something out of this."

"Why do you think that?"

"Because, otherwise, you wouldn't do it."

"I heal people," I blurted out. "Is it so wrong to want

to protect others?"

"A thieving pirate captain with blood on his name?" Hook asked as if to remind me. *Like I could ever forget.* His eyes narrowed. "Unless there's more you aren't telling me?"

"I told you everything you need to know."

There was a snicker, and both of us snapped towards the sound to find Piper standing in the doorway. Rats made more noise when moving about. He glanced away, hand briefly lifted as if silently asking for a pardon. "Just wanted to say that I'm leaving to stay on shore."

"I should go as well." Discussing everything regarding the pirates could be sorted out later when I was in a better frame of mind. My head was too cloudy being around Captain Hook so much lately.

I stepped out first, squeezing between Piper and the doorway, and made for the dock. It wasn't dry land but just being off the boat should help. As if also eager to abandon ship, Piper followed. I shot him a harsh questioning glance, and he all but ignored it.

"What? I also prefer land."

Piper moved behind me like a shadow before I stopped to turn to him fully around the marketplace. "What do you want?"

"A job."

I looked over at him for the first time. It took a second to consider him as just a passenger instead of on Hook's crew. He didn't look the part of a pirate with his clothes more suited for cold weather than the seawater.

"It's been all volunteers since the Queen left," I finally said.

"Aw, fuck'n 'ell." Piper glanced around, sucking air

through his teeth and seeming to not know where to go. "Where does one go for work in this damn place?"

Seeing him as his own person made it easy to find him earnest, which made me smile a little. "You swear like a sailor. Sure you aren't one?"

"Absolutely am not," Piper groaned. "Just got lured on board with the promise of gold and a blow before."

"Excuse me?" I laughed at his candor.

"Not from Hook," Piper said and playfully bumped into my shoulder. "In case you were worried."

He was way too outgoing for my anxiety today, but he seemed friendly enough that I didn't want to be rude either. "So, you're a summoner? I haven't seen any in a long time, and then suddenly two came to town."

Piper shrugged. "Not like there's a connection. I can summon wind and a few animals. The music makes the magic influence more powerful."

"That's pretty cool." I didn't catch what the other mage's specialty was, but I knew there was something wrong with how he drew on magic. Piper, however, was far more playful.

"Makes rat-catching easier, but it's not making-someone-nigh-immortal cool."

I frowned suddenly, almost embarrassed that another mage knew about that. "Has magic ever just... slipped out of your hands before?"

Piper's gaze grew unfocused. "My first love said I'd hum this hypnotic tune—wouldn't even realize I was doing it until he pulled close and kissed me. He always said it was the best way to get me to stop."

Wistfully, I glanced back at the ship over the shoulder towards the water. "Where is he now?"

"Beats me," Piper said, and I noticed that his eyes stayed facing forward. The man who convinced him to come aboard might not even be there anymore. "Said my first love, not my last. The thing he adored in me originally grew to annoy him." When a frown started to set on my face, Piper was quick to speak again. "I don't think Hook is like that. He revels in what you do to him."

"That's not—" After a steadying breath, I just shook my head.

The quickest way to stop thinking about Hook was to stop talking about him. It wasn't like he was just some guy. There was no chance of just having fun and going our separate ways to never really think of or care about again. Magic had upped the stakes, and without caution, I could irreparably harm pieces of our souls. A part that rested deep inside and would be impossible to heal.

"Are you going to follow me all day?"

"Huh?" Piper glanced around and realized we were halfway to the castle. "Wow, I should pay better attention to where I'm going. No work further your way?"

I shook my head. "Not the type that could pay you in blow jobs either." The words felt awkward in my mouth. It wasn't not my usual humor, but Piper cracked up, making the attempt worth it.

"You're fun. Thought you'd be stuffy."

My smile stayed put but gained a nervous waiver. I definitely would consider myself more stiff than lively company.

Before I thought of it too much, Piper nodded towards the castle. "Since I'm staying in town, hopefully, I'll see you around more?"

"Yeah, maybe."

CHAPTER EIGHT
— HOOK —

"Remember me?" Warren once asked softly. One eye shifted from a stunning golden brown to the color of forget-me-nots. *How could I not?* He felt like my missing half. It had been many moons since he first had said that, and that man remained what I wanted to possess the most.

Before, I could convince myself that once I fucked him, the siren-like lure to this coast would lessen. Now, the desire to be around was crystal clear. It wasn't this town, dock, beach, or wild magic. *It was him.*

And I couldn't even leave the ship to say as much. The cost for his magical protection was that my legs were no good on land when the moon was full. I'd even be wobbly on the docks like how some men got from being out at sea for too long. But, unlike them, only the changing phase of the moon would make the difference.

"You upset about that mage?" Smee asked, offering over the spyglass. Her main focus was on the horizon along with mine.

I grunted a reply. Neither Warren nor Piper had returned, and not answering kept things vague. "How's the weather looking?"

"Without a favorable wind, we might need to wait an

extra day to avoid the worst of a storming brewing." Smee turned fully towards me. "Shall I go collect Piper? I'm sure more gold would convince him of another voyage with us."

"Aye. Might as well offer."

Smee didn't leave right away, and my eyes fell towards her in question.

"Shall I kidnap the other mage as well?"

"Wouldn't that be something," I said with a wicked grin. The idea was delightful, but not actually what I wanted. "Leave him be. He'll come when he wants."

"Aye, Captain."

— WARREN —

When I told Piper we might see each other soon, I hadn't expected him to show up at our doorstep and push past Jonathan, demanding I save him from pirates. To be fair, I wasn't not sure what I had expected either. He was as colorful with words as the clothes he wore.

Piper snapped his fingers to catch my attention across the room even before I had the chance to cross it. "Warren! There you are. I need help; Smee is trying to convince me to go back out to sea."

I glanced towards Jonathan who had been minding the door, as Sophie lifted her head from her studies. Smiling to them both softly, I said I'd take care of whatever this was.

"Just tell them no?" I offered Piper once it was just us.

"I can't. The pay is too good—unless *you* can outbid

them."

"Things have not changed within the day since we talked. You can stay here if you wish, but there's no job here for you." My eyes caught the musical instrument on his belt, and I realized that I didn't even know this mage's real name.

Piper seemed undeterred or, at least, unaware of my growing suspicions of him. "Don't you own this castle? Surely you can find something old and valuable to offer me in exchange for... I don't know—cleaning something."

I wasn't sure where he heard that bit of truth, but there was no sense in denying it now. "The things here aren't mine to give you. They were the Queen's. If anything, they now belong to everyone."

"Then let me take my pick," Piper whined, "I'm so tired of being out on a ship."

"No," I said firmly. And to my happy surprise, Piper hung his head and sighed. There was always value in someone who listened when told to stop. "Look, I need to talk to Captain Hook anyway. Maybe... you can become the college's liaison to the pirates? Would that make everyone happy?"

"Sounds perfect to me!" Piper held his hand out flat as if waiting for payment. When I did nothing but stare, he lifted his hand and pointed to it with the other. "High five?"

"Oh!"

He got his high five a little late, and our hands made a loud crisp clap as I tried to make up for the delay with enthusiasm.

"Yeah! Collective worker's rights or what-the-fuck-ever!" Piper said cheerfully and headed towards the door.

"I don't work for the pirates!"

"Uh-huh," Piper said, disbelief all too clear as he held the door for me to follow. "Labor is labor. Time to work out your payment."

Huh, I didn't think I disagreed. With haste, I told Jonathan I wouldn't be long and waved goodbye to Sophie before catching up with Piper. I didn't know how he could have any idea what he signed himself up for since I had just made a position up on the spot. But he truly did not seem to care as long as it paid well enough.

Smee glared as we showed up together. I was pretty sure I somehow complicated something she had been told to do, but she was too tightlipped to clarify as to what. She rested a hand on her sword before she dramatically sighed. "Fine, but you need to discuss this with the Captain. Come with me."

"Bring the Captain out," Piper said, holding his ground. I didn't think Hook could given the phase of his water-locked curse, but I held my tongue, curious to see what would happen.

Smee grumbled to herself before letting another "fine" slip between her lips. A moment later, Hook came out on deck but didn't venture a foot off the *Jolly Roger*. He shifted uncomfortably before addressing us. "You both wanted to talk?"

"We want to stay on land," Piper yelled up towards him.

His gaze slid off to the musician like water and flowed to me. "I don't care all that much for Piper's objection since a few coins easily overcome it. But we still have business to discuss. However, I'm itching to set sail. Since you are here, may we go around the bay as we four discuss?"

"And return later today?" I asked.

"Aye."

He did look uneasy and hadn't pushed the topic, so I figured this would be a fair compromise. "Okay, deal."

Our talks about employment and trade quickly became hard to follow since Smee wanted to focus on Piper's ability to control the weather. The rest of the crew shifted into a frenzied focus to get the *Jolly Roger* ready to set sail. Hook and I weren't discussing anything personal, which was preferable. Things like giving Piper more shore time while the crew was swapped out from their light duty of watching over the castle. If this pace kept up, we'd be sailing all night.

"Can we break this up into groups?"

Hook smiled at my words, looking more interested than he had been. From his point of view, it must've been a banner day already. We were gliding over the water, and I had yet to throw up as I once claimed I would. "If you wish to discuss privately, we could go up to the crow's nest."

I glanced up at it, suddenly worried my lie over motion sickness would turn into a very real fear of heights.

"Unless my quarters are better?" Hook smirked.

"Crow's nest is fine."

Smee continued to glare at Piper who had already gotten his usual rate doubled. I was worried she might push him overboard, but he looked very pleased, so I left his business to him and started to climb up the mast.

Hook followed, making quick time up, and settled into a lean against the wooden railing as I was stunned over the view. We hadn't sailed far but even in the short time, the land looked so different from this distance away. And if I looked towards him, there was nothing but blue water and sky.

"You have an odd way of going about things," I said.

"Too many people suffer under the law, so I made sure I sail clear of it." His tone was guarded, and I wondered if the spell tugged at him too.

Maybe we both weren't telling the other about the underlying feelings. "Are you feeling better?"

He nodded, before pulling back his expression into something more neutral. "I need the ocean sea like most pirates want rum. Better alone on the seas than a clueless fool bending to the whim of landowners."

I frowned, not following who he was complaining about. "Is that what you think I do? Do you even know what you are searching for out here?"

"No." His gaze lowered to his boots, and I thought that was it until his lips parted. "Yet, there's a compulsion to keep looking until I find ...*something*."

Maybe I should tell him that what he is searching for might be me. Could I be causing him restlessness by resisting what I felt? "James—"

"Yes?" His eyes softened in a way that had nothing to do with magic, and it rippled a weakness in me that scared me.

I cleared my throat and nod my chin towards the ocean. "What's that?"

Hook stepped forward to lean on the other side of the crow's nest, squinting to make out the small shape floating on the water. "Driftwood, probably."

Piper and Smee were below us, standing apart from the rest of the crew we all discussed. One of them was having fun, and it was clearly still Piper. I breathed in deep. The ship was moving fast enough that the wind was whipping my hair around. Even the scent was just different out there. Less smoke, dirt, and moss.

"It's truly something up here. I didn't expect to feel so..."

"Free?" Hook offered.

I shook my head and turned away from the land to look at the endless ocean. My gaze skimmed over the water until it hit the horizon and pulled up towards the full moon above us. "A part of something bigger. I thought the sea would make me feel lonely."

"What do you want?" Hook's voice called from behind me.

I closed my eyes, trying to focus. "I want the castle to be safe enough that education can happen there."

"No. I asked what do *you* want. I'm not asking about your job or desired location. What do you want for yourself, Warren?"

With a look over my shoulder, I found myself distracted and content simply to appreciate his handsome face for longer. "I want to be with a nice man."

"No, you don't," Hook laughed, dismissing the very idea. "You're already a nice man. Another wouldn't compliment you. You need a man who will fight *for* you, not with you."

"Is that man you?" I asked, fearing he knew the truth I learned long ago.

Hook's shoulders shrugged briefly, the metal of his

hand glinting in the light. "Could be."

I licked my lips and didn't look away. "What's out there anyway?"

"The Neverlands."

If we went where time stopped, could I not only hold onto how I felt, but indulge in it too?

"Captain!" Smee yelled up from the deck below. "We have a deal if you approve."

"Aye, we'll see!" Hook shouted back before he started to climb down.

I shook my head, trying not to think of myself. Then, I followed to hear whatever Smee and Piper had worked out. To my surprise, Piper had the college in mind when discussing. Apparently, after hearing the intent of having a mage college in the first place, he wanted to help. The King's dream had come to rest solely on me, but maybe a small fraction rested with Piper now too. He just didn't want himself, or anyone, to work for free. And as much as pirates seemed to love rum, they also liked coming back alive to enjoy more of it. Piper could help them do that.

"Let's drink to our partnership!" Smee said, sloshing rum into four different cups for us and handing one to each of us.

With a drink in hand, I lifted it towards the trio. "Let's drink to our health."

"Hear, hear!" Piper cheered. "To our good fortunes."

Hook was the only one who stayed silent, not lifting his cup until my eyes caught his. "To you," he said, before breaking the red hot intensity his gaze held as he downed the rum.

CHAPTER NINE
— HOOK —

Piper played music for everyone's enjoyment today. It didn't take much to spur the crew into a shanty in the first place, all but eager to provide lyrics over the folk notes from his pipe. Smee sat near, tapping a steady beat against a barrel.

Being tone-deaf left me silently watching their enjoyment. I doubted Warren had the same problem; maybe he just lacked the words to follow along as he sat on a few crates that the crew hadn't pulled off the ship to sell quite yet.

"You should move off of those so the crew doesn't forget them today," I said, stepping close to tug off a label we hadn't spotted beforehand. This extended stay at the port was making people careless.

"You should check your men for scurvy more often."

I shot him an accusatory look that he must have read as confusion because he gestured towards his teeth.

"Are you suggesting I should target orange shipments next?"

"I'm not suggesting you steal anything."

My eyes narrowed at the mage. Maybe a college was needed since I hadn't a damn clue how his healing abilities worked. Or how any of the mages aboard did what they did. "If the crew got scurvy, couldn't you just heal them?"

Warren shook his head. "I can't cure deficiencies caused by a diet. The elements have to be within the body for me to control it."

I tugged on the piercing in my ear, holding back the wariness settling into my chest. "So, in your medical option, you are suggesting what?"

"Become blimey limeys? You have enough money to pay Piper and the rest of the crew. Simply buy more fruit?"

My hand fell away from my face. "Warren, darling. Where do you think we get money from?"

He scoffed. "This conversation feels like it's becoming a circular firing squad. I don't even remember why we are arguing."

"I asked you to move off the stolen crates of tea. You made a comment about juice which got us here."

"Oh." Warren finally pushed himself off the crate he was sitting on. "Sorry. I'm not the crew's doctor, and I think I forget to turn some thoughts off when trying to socialize."

"Why don't you hang out with Piper while we finish unloading?" I motioned over to the other mage.

Piper's name on my tongue caught the musician's attention since his part of the song had finished. "Pass," he said, turning to look over his shoulder as if to take a glance at what he exactly dismissed. "Yeah, no. I don't want to get involved with your awkward lover's quell."

"We're not—" Warren and I started at the same time. And neither of us dared to clarify if we were going to claim lack of awkwardness or being lovers.

The wind tugged open a seam line of the jib sail as we were sailing around the port to see if the repairs would hold up to heavier wind. Piper had disembarked, but to my surprise, Warren had stayed on board for the afternoon.

He was currently leaning over the side of the ship, watching the comparative shallows and the different creatures that lived just outside his usual life. I thought about tugging him back to his feet, but his soft curious smile stayed my hand.

I stood next to him, near enough to catch him if he were to fall overboard. An octopus slid among rocks lining the bay's floor. You'd never see larger animals this close to shore, but it was the perfect depth for smaller curiosities.

When the same fish passed twice, Warren glanced over at me. "Thank you for being around as long as you have. I know a lot of plans had to be made—all involving a lot of people to rotate the crews out for the college's protection."

"Of course." Being Captain wasn't the type of job that came with many thanks. You got paid in respect which was a different currency. "Plus, if you look at the bright side, now we won't ever be out long enough for anyone to be lacking citrus."

Warren didn't seem to find the humor and winched more than he smiled. "I hate fighting about things that don't matter. But there is something I need to tell you first if we are ever going to be together."

There's nothing I feared on the ocean anymore, but that distant feeling crept back in. "What is it?"

"So, um..." His hand nervously lifted to the side of his

head and fingered the single braid of his hair that held any length. There was a story there I had yet to discover. "As a child, the Queen thought I was a woman."

"Oh?" I thought I understood what he was trying to tell me, but I also didn't want to cut him off before he was finished speaking. "And I'm assuming you corrected her?"

Warren nodded, biting down on his lip, and looked far more nervous than what was needed with me. "Then I healed myself. Does that... change how you feel about me?"

If I followed the same logic from earlier about curing an outside issue with what was already within, there was enough shared understanding that I didn't need time or anything to accept this. It was easy.

"It doesn't change anything for me." I cupped Warren's face in my hand, running my thumb under his chin. How other people incorrectly saw him wasn't a valid concern. What mattered was I knew and adored the truth. "I already think you're amazing and deserve better than what people have given you in life thus far. You're wondrous."

"You think so?"

"Aye, 'tis clear as day."

CHAPTER TEN
– HOOK –

Ships in the harbor were safe, but that was not what ships were built for. I wasn't quite sure if Warren realized that since, every evening after his chores, he'd wander down to the docks and onto the ship to mingle with the crew.

A full moon provided plenty of light for people to travel between the ship, pier, and tavern as they pleased. Since magic had 'cursed' me to stay on the water, there was nowhere on land for me to go. I hadn't ever minded until that darling man proved to be within a walking distance. What would happen when soil no longer connected our worlds?

Being as subtle as a bull, I twirled my gun up from my belt and held it out flat in my palm for him to take. "If you are ever going to travel with us, you should know how to use this."

With a curious expression as if unsure of what exactly he wanted to object over, Warren picked up the pistol. "Does the crew get into that many scraps?"

"You never know what the future holds."

A frown was clear on his face, but he nodded and conceded the point at least.

I gestured towards the railing where I had lined up a few empty rum bottles with more targets waiting beneath.

Warren aimed, moving down the line from target to target, but he didn't fire.

"Your grip is too tight. It makes your movement rigid and without flow."

"I know how bodies work." Warren's tone had a biting edge before he lowered the pistol to the ground and turned toward me. "I'm sorry. I don't mean to take my mood out on you."

Life at sea with a crew that could range from drunk, tired, injured, or all three at once made people snappy. No pirate could afford to take it personally. Instead, I crossed my arms over my chest and tried to appraise him. "Why are you then?"

Warren brought the gun up enough to look at it in his hand. "This feels like a game. Like a ruse to get closer to me. I'm so used to fighting that instinct that the knee-jerk reaction is still right there."

I smiled, both guilty of what he accused me of and happy he told me. My guess would have been that as a healer, he didn't like the idea of harming someone. "Gun or not, if you desired, you probably could be the deadliest on board. Chest compressions can break ribs. It's not hard to imagine what else you could do if you wanted to break bones rather than mend them."

Warren nodded, lifting the pistol once again towards the bottles. His aim held steady on a bottle, giving me a moment to give his stance a critical eye.

"Relax your arm a little," I offered. "You don't want the kickback to hurt."

Warren glanced over to where I was standing. A slight smile sparked to life after I raised a brow. "Lucky for you, I do prefer this game more than some of your others," he said. Then, he looked back and fired. The bottle shattered and pulled my attention away from his handsome face. "Eyes on the target," he seemed to say to himself.

"Aye." As Warren aimed the gun toward the second bottle, I moved to stand behind him, my chest pressed to his back like two magnets aligning. His eyes closed as if breathing me in. I leaned in, resisting the urge to taste him, and whispered into his ear, "You'll need to act quicker in battle."

He fired again. The glass broke in an instant, raining down into the water below. "Maybe if you weren't distracting me so."

"Maybe." The warmth of my breath bounced off his delicious neck.

The pistol lowered as his weight swayed into me. "I feel so lovesick and fear you might need to put me out of my misery."

"I get to heal the healer?" What a delightful prospect. I lowered my mouth on his neck, feeling his heart race under my lips as I kissed at his pulse. "Pretty sure you're owed some bliss."

He turned in my arms as I guided us towards the edge of the ship. Glass crunched under our boots. And it was by sound and position that I realized he'd put the pistol down along the side before pulling himself up. A soft splash followed as he bumped the last bottle off.

"Here?" I laughed softly, barely pulling back to speak even as my hand anchored his face up to me.

"It's your ship, is it not?" Warren dared.

"You wicked little thing. Will I ever tire of the words that come out of that mouth of yours?" I didn't allow Warren to even answer as I slid my tongue into his mouth, kissing him with enough pent-up passion that his arms wrap around my neck to hold on.

I kneed his legs apart so I could press our bodies even closer. Warren tilted his head back, outstretching his neck and becoming too much of a temptation for my mouth to not wander there.

"Who cares if we are star-crossed," Warren mumbled after a pleased sigh. "Fate was right about us."

For all the musing about destiny, something feels off. Not quite sure what, I grew still. Tensing up as Warren pulled back to study my expression. As if looking to heal some injury I've caused myself.

"What's wrong?" he asked.

My chest grew tight as I stepped back to untangle myself from him. "These... feelings I have towards you are because of magic?"

"No. It's not like that." Warren took a breath trying to gather his thoughts. If we were drawn together, I couldn't understand how he hadn't thought out this exact conversation beforehand. "Fuck, I should have said something sooner. My mentor told me before I ever saw you that we were fated for each other."

"You knew this the whole time?" My hand rubbed my chest. Feeling a tinge of pain there that his magic wasn't equipped to protect me from.

Warren flinched at the volume of my voice. "Yes."

"I don't even believe in fate! What I trusted was *you*. Was my future just a plaything? Someone you cast out to sea simply to see how many times the tide brought me back to you? Knowing according to your faith that I had no choice?"

"No! I swear it's not like that." Warren pushed himself off the railing. When I took another step back to maintain a distance, he stopped with a frown. "James... please. Let me explain."

"It's Captain Hook," I said, biting back. "You had your chance to explain the spell to me plenty, but you refused because you didn't *want* me to know. Get off my ship."

Smee stepped up from below the deck. Her gaze originally moved over us as if expecting someone new given the raised voices. "Something wrong, Captain?"

"No. Warren was just leaving." I didn't look back at him, afraid of what I might feel if I had. Freedom was the only thing I believed in. *How dare he keep this secret.* Smee held my hard gaze, silently asking for orders. "Let everyone know we set sail in the morning."

CHAPTER ELEVEN
- WARREN -

What was the point of staying home when it was so empty? I opted to just walk into the marketplace hoping to find something that stirred any other feeling from me besides the deep regret in my chest.

A few pleasantries were exchanged, and I offered a cheerful smile that paled in comparison to the true version given to me. Instead of pacing down the long length of shops for a second time, I just sat down by a bench that marked the end of the shops.

Shadows shifted on the cobblestone in front of me as a man sat down. I blinked over at the figure in surprise. "Piper? Why aren't you on the ship?"

"Didn't you listen to me before? I don't like traveling by boat." His voice wasn't harsh as he casually stretched his legs out. "Why do you look so down?"

"Hook left."

Piper titled his head, not seeing the problem because I once again left key details out. "Doesn't he every month?"

I nodded and turned my attention forward. "Guess I should be happy that he'll likely be back." Maybe I should tell Piper the truth as well. Would Captain Hook be upset I was discussing him, or could it be the start of me admitting how I felt about things? "Everyone needs healing at some point, right?"

Piper rolled his eyes. "Yeah, your *spell* is why he keeps coming back here."

I tensed and shifted how I was sitting trying to find the comfort I had lost at sea. As I looked back at Piper, I was tempted to just walk away, and the thought that I still could somehow gave me the courage to speak. "Why are you mocking me?"

He leaned back on the bench, pulling an arm up to rest against the back. "I'm mostly mocking Hook—if it helps."

"Not really."

"Then, tell me," Piper said. "What's different now?"

I explained everything. Although some of it felt out of order and almost sadder than I had realized at the time. Still, it was the truth, and that had to count for something.

"Wait," Piper said, after nothing more than a nod to show he was listening. "So how did you know you and Hook were fated for each other?"

"There used to be another mage here. She told me that I'd find my soul mate if I stayed, that we were destined for each other, and I would know him by his brown and blue eyes. She'd seen that one of mine change when I cast. It was enough of an oddity that I thought she was just using that detail to convince me. Never thought I'd run across someone like that or feel anything if I did."

"Until Hook," Piper finished the thought.

"Yeah, but no one told him, not even me. Until yesterday."

"Ah," Piper breathed out. "And what made you sure it wasn't just a coincidence after all?"

What harm was there in confessing now? At least someone would know my feelings on the matter, even if it wasn't exactly who I wanted. "It was after I had cast the protection spell when he lost his hand. I started to hear his voice in the wind and felt pulled out to sea even when I knew his ship wasn't near."

Piper hummed his agreement along with a nod. "And now Hook's upset because he feels like his attraction is no different than a compass arrow pointing towards an unchangeable north."

My shoulders deflated with a heavy sigh. "Suppose so."

"Well, that's stupid."

His words were so simple and absolute sounding that they left me lightheaded. My chest tightened with embarrassment for having told him anything at all.

"We are both mages," Piper said, unaware of the effect he had on me, "and I know how magic sings to people. But the romantic artists got a key tenet of their philosophy wrong. There's no such thing as true individualism. We are all pulled together and pushed apart by the notes that came before and the ones we play after. What compels people is what they feel. Emotion is the law of the soul. Seize your heartbreak. Play your future out."

My lips parted, but I was left stunned beyond words to reply. Fate may have given me this hand, but *I* was the one who had refused to ever go all in. The moment the Wolf King offered some alternate, grander future, I bought into that noble dream instead.

"You're right." I said and stood up.

"Wait!" Piper called. "Do you truly know what Hook's like out on the seas? What any of the pirates are like?"

I turned back with a small smile. Witnessing them firsthand wasn't needed because I had caught it in their eyes—seen it in mine first. There was the realization that monsters hide under children's beds because they feared facing the rest of mankind. Out of every creature on land, sea, or air, humans were the only ones that delighted in the torment of another. Even loving communities could foster harmful seeds and have it take take root. *But did Piper see?*

"Why do you ask?"

He shrugged, even as his lip twitched. A tick that suggested he did care. "Don't want to do you a favor that you'll end up regretting."

That was a kindness that felt rare. "You're a nice man, Piper."

"Yeah?" He asked with a laugh. "Well, don't tell anyone. Nice earns lower pay."

"Ah," I said, laughing along with him. "Your game entails traveling with pirates to imply you have their strong-armed loyalty."

"Do you want me to summon the pirates?" Piper asked.

"Can you?" As soon as the words left my mouth, I knew this was what I had wanted for myself.

"Aye." Piper stared up at me for a moment before he held up a hand for my help. I took it and pulled him to his feet. "Would you like to know what magic sings to me about you?"

My breath grew shaky. I felt wildly close to him in this movement even after I had stepped back to a respectful distance. But it wasn't love or lust filling the distance between us. It was kinship. Words failed me, and all I could do was nod.

His focus lingered on me as if needing to first listen. "A healer's hands must accept the blood needed to mend the broken bones of the world."

"That's lovely." *And tragic.* Piper must have a bard's soul in order to keep his humor intact whilst traveling with pirates and struggling to find work. A softer center that kept him from truly falling in with the crew or growing love for the dark depth of the sea.

For him to even be able to safely summon the *Jolly Roger,* or her crew, they must be connected somehow. Given I had harmed Captain Hook with the suggestion that he didn't have a choice, it felt wrong to demand he return so soon.

"Could you wait?" I asked.

Piper raised a brow. "Wanting to see if love returns on its own first?"

A jolt of panic washed over me. *That was exactly what I wanted.*

It was days after the waxing crescent moon, and a quarter moon hung in the sky above. My anxiety had been unbearable for the last few days. I had led Piper to the beach over to where I felt the pull would be strongest and better allow for the notes to carry.

We stood on a rocky outcrop that overlooked the ocean. Piper took a careful look over the jagged rocks that turned even the calmest waves harsh. "You've got an artist's eye," he said with a step back. "And a bloody romantic soul."

He lifted his pipe and began to play. It wasn't a song I've heard him perform before, but there was a buzz underneath it I've heard plenty. Each note was dipped with magic, making his beautiful notes haunting as if something lived within the sound.

I listened to him play all night until the sun started to tint the water a wondrous orange hue, seeing no sails on the horizon but feeling far less alone.

CHAPTER TWELVE
– HOOK –

A siren song rattled around in my skull with a magnetic pull that whispered, *"to shore - to shore - to shore."* If the wind hadn't been at our back, I may have thrown myself overboard, convinced I could swim there faster. My heart hammered in my chest, beating hard enough that a phantom pain ran down my arm stopping past where the hook had replaced my lost hand.

I might skin that musical mage once we got to the marina. To summon the *Jolly Roger* this way was the type of witchcraft that made people despise their abilities. Worse yet was the beauty in the notes that drew me close. *A moth happy to burn.*

Two figures stood out on the farthest pier, and I yelled to the crew to bring us around. The tension in the ropes could be heard as they stained to close the sails against the wind in the masts pushing us further. The crew yelled to each other, chains clanked and knots creaked as the ship rocked to a stop.

I disembarked from the ship before the momentum had even settled. "Stop that insistent song already!"

Piper quickly did and stepped back. He even moved his instrument behind him as if fearing I might snap it in two.

Warren stood firm as I stormed over, only speaking

once I was close enough that he didn't have to yell. "Apologies, Captain. We needed you to return posthaste." Warren swallowed roughly and raised his chin trying to fake confidence that didn't make it past a tremor in his voice. "You left some men behind. Piper, and... *me*."

The song had left my head, and all that remained was the call of the birds above and an echo of the pain over how the two of us left things. "We are days off the usual schedule. Do you mean to enforce a curfew?"

Warren's gaze fell away, seeming as terrified of me as he had been when we first met. "Piper convinced me this was the best course."

"Hey! Dick move." Piper rolled his eyes at Warren before pulling on a smile as he spoke to me. "As for my part in this, it's been over two weeks, and there's truly no jobs here. I want a ride somewhere else, and your crew still has my shares."

For someone who never seemed to be able to get his sea legs, Piper sure had the gold-loving heart of a pirate. Annoyed with them both, I glared knowing he'd get bored first and get on with the rest of it.

"*Oh-kay*, I see you aren't in a talkative mood," Piper continued. "Allow me to speed this along as well. Warren here wouldn't shut up about how heartbroken he felt. And now will do the grown-up thing of using his words."

"I will?" Warren asked, face going as pale as the sand before he nodded. "I will."

Granting a smile was the last thing I wanted to offer him, but he was truly under my skin in a wonderfully impossible way that made me anyway.

"Captain Hook," Warren said, licking lips I couldn't pull my gaze from. "Please, forgive the insult to your freedom. Hurting you is the last thing I wanted. After getting to know you, I truly believe that if I had told you the day we meant, you would have laughed at the suggestion of fate and acted the same towards me. If anything these past two weeks apart should help me prove my magic doesn't have control of your own choices. That's why Piper had to play the summoning request."

"I didn't think fondly about you while away," I said, harsher than I intended. A stuttering breath was stolen from Warren's lungs upon hearing the words.

"Kindly fuck yourself, Captain," Piper scolded before I could finish. "Why are you two like this? Both of you need to stop being so terrified to love each other. Who cares if it's fate or just chance? You look at Warren and tell me you didn't just lash out and hurt both of you in the process."

"I didn't think fondly at all," I repeated, directly to Warren again, "because I ended up hating myself so much more. Trying to dislike you was so against my nature that it felt like trying to drown myself. I couldn't even get rid of your paintings because I saw the same longing you had poured into them within myself."

"Step away from the Captain, Piper," Smee yelled from behind me. "Give them a moment."

I glanced back towards her as she watched from the ship, and I grinned over the support of the whole crew that was needed to get us here. When my focus turned back to Warren, he was giving Piper an encouraging nod that it was okay.

I moved closer, feeling drawn to him even without any magic sizzling on my skin or upon the wind. "Shall I take this all as a confession that you've missed me?"

Warren stood there as if in shock before suddenly colliding into me with a hug. He shook hard enough that he probably was crying as I wrapped my arms around him.

"I thought you might never come back."

"I'm sorry, darling." I cupped his cheek and whipped away a single lingering tear with my thumb.

"I'm so relieved." He pulled back just enough to look up at me, and I was appalled that I had ever let go. "I didn't think words, or the song were going to be enough, so I did more." Warren stepped away to pull out some papers from a bag sitting on the ground. "It's the deed for the castle. The King gave them to me to prove his sincerity. I thought I could use it to prove mine to you." He ripped the papers in half before letting the wind blow the pieces apart. "Who needs land when I'm this close to the one thing I want in life for myself?"

I watched the papers as they landed on the surface of the water and floated as the ink dissolved into a black blotch. "Why did you do that? I came back."

"I know. And I won't ask you to stay. Instead... take me with you?" My gaze snapped back to find Warren as he finished speaking. "I could be a pirate. Good in a fight— that is, if you'd want that."

Skepticism fought with surprise over which would be expressed first, ending in me muttering sound without much meaning. "Your dream of a school?"

"Only landlords value deeds," Warren explained. "With no royals and a disbanded guard, who is left to take the castle from anyone living there? Especially with the pirate's protection. Establishing a college for mages doesn't have to be my everything."

"And your friends?"

"Sophie and Jonathan are their own people," Warren said fondly, "who will carry on our shared hope, or they may move on to find what they need to be happy."

I seized a kiss that made Warren's knees weak and

steadied him against me with a hand on his lower back. When we parted, he stared up at my mismatched eyes. "I love you, Warren. Not for how you protect me, but how you care about everyone—for the stunning things you create from yourself to your paintings. You're the best thing that's ever happened to me, and I desperately want to be the same for you."

"I love you too." He lifted on his feet, pressing his mouth against mine as if determined to back up every word with action.

Piper wolf-whistled, and Warren flipped him off only to get a laugh. Without another word, I scooped Warren up in my arms.

"Whoa," he laughed. "Where are we going?"

"You're coming to live with me. Any objections?"

"My bag." Warren stretched an arm out towards it.

I reached out an arm and caught the strap with my hook. "If there's no spare canvas in here, I'm stealing the first roll I see."

He laughed softly next to my ear. "How could you be any more perfect for me?"

"If you think of a way, let me know," I said and carried him back to the boat.

"Hey, guys?" Piper called as he ran over to catch up to us. "I can come too, right? I was hoping I could pick where we go next since I helped stage this."

Once on the ship, I placed Warren down and signaled to the rest of the crew that we would set sail soon either way. "What do you think, darling?"

"I, for one," Warren said, "will forever be grateful for his support."

Piper pumped a fist in the air. "Woo, mage solidarity!"

He was worthy of a laugh, but I also quickly wanted to make him Smee's problem instead. "Go tell my first mate where you want to go."

Piper scanned the crew for her and headed over to lie on the charm as if all a fun game.

Warren shook his head at the scene. "Maybe you should be more careful ruling in my favor. Who knows where he will take us."

"Aye," I laughed. "But, can't say I care as long as it's together."

His eyes seemed to light up with joy as he took his bag from me, looping it over his shoulder before returning his empty hand to mine.

"Would you like a tour of the ship?"

"Yes, please."

"Correct reply on a ship is 'aye.'"

"Aye," Warren repeated with a dangerous little edge I wanted to sharpen. "My captain, my love; show me this giant *ship* of yours."

"A filthy comment. You're going to make a fine pirate."

"I have a confession," Warren said as he settled his things into my cabin.

"Another?" I tried to hold back my tone, but I've never been all that good at it, and the word came out like a warning.

"It's about magic," he said and nodded toward my hook. "And your hand."

Warren had shut down when stuff became difficult before, so it hardly seems right to shut him down now.

"I never told you about how the spell worked because... I was afraid that you'd be able to convince me we were meant for each other—that I'd give up everything before I was ready. You're the only person who never made me feel like I wasn't enough. You were the only other person who saw healing as something that comes *after* an injury and not as a reversal. All you asked was for the pain to stop. That's a level of acceptance that's so precious when I can even make a silent heart beat.

"And then," Warren added with a nervous laugh. "You told me your name because you didn't want me to fear you. I knew it was a hidden treasure to know you like that. I had never believed in the prophecy before that, but right then, I knew what a good man you were. I just couldn't let anything happen to you, and I hate how I was the one to hurt you."

"You protected far more than you ever harmed." I couldn't count the number of times I'd been reckless because of his safety net. "I can't promise we won't ever upset each other again. But, I do promise to always give you the best I have to offer."

Warren nodded. "Sounds fair. I'm happy to pull my weight here. Does your ship have a surgeon?"

"Are you good with a needle?"

"Why?" he teased, breaking into a soft smile. "Need another tattoo instead?"

"Will you ever cease to amaze me?"

"I hope not." He leaned in close, and we softly kissed as if both now believing there'd be plenty of time.

CHAPTER THIRTEEN
— WARREN —

Sink or swim was not an option here. A rough wave pounded against the hull, splashing up over the desk as rain battered down on the ship. The sky was dark as the water broke out of its usual calm with a choppy swell.

Hook held onto the wheel as it attempted to twist and spin free on his control. His jaw was set over the storm being rougher than usual. I blinked up at the rain that had already left everyone soaked through. Piper's music cut in and out of it all, unable to hold a solid beat as the wild magic fought against both of their attempts to sail out of the harsh weather.

A shout came from above as one of the riggers wavered and was pushed off balance by the wind. A rope caught around his ankle before another rough wave knocked him free as he fell to the deck below. He coughed up blood. The droplets spit up only to speckle down on his mouth.

I rushed over, taking his hand in mine to see if he has any strength to grip back or even pull away. "What's your name?"

He looked wide-eyed and afraid. "Mack."

"Mack," I repeated with an encouraging smile. "Did you bite your tongue?"

The pirate blinked up as if confused before his lips parted as if to check where his pain is located. "Yeah, my back hurts too."

"I got you, Mack." I pulled my hand free and hovered it over his chest drawing up magic so I can feel exactly where in his back. Low in his spine. I could sense a compression fracture in a vertebra. Afraid to move him, I drew on magic to repair it, and the thread of healing snagged against all the magic from the storm. I pushed through and gasped as my vision cut in half.

"Bless you. Thank you," Mack panted.

With a nod, I pushed on toward his ankle. Not being paralyzed was a brilliant first step, but if he couldn't stand, then he was still a sitting duck out in this storm. Before I could even cast again, a wave swept over the deck.

"Find another way," Hook yelled. "The magic in the storm is too unpredictable to sail if you snare it again."

Right, I could do this. Keeping my balance was tricky, but I managed to grab some bandages from my covered bag. He was already pulling off his boot, so I quickly went to work wrapping his foot—first under the toes and then figure-eights up until reaching his ankle where I secured the bandage with a final loop.

Mack moved to stand up, using me as a backup in case his ankle was worse than it seemed. With a nod of thanks, his hands moved to the ship itself as he slowly guided himself below deck.

"Your eyes are still two-toned." Hook's own darkened, the intensity making my heart race ever faster. "Are you okay, Warren?"

My name on his lips settled the last of my frayed nerves, even as my vision remained out of focus. "It should stop once we are out of the storm."

"Aye." Hook spun the wheel around and pressed the advantage of the favorable winds Piper gained, and with a small hitch from a wave, the ship settled out in calm waters. The fellow mage slid down against the wooden wall behind him as if calling it quits.

My eyes came back into sync with each other, and I made my way over to him. "Hanging in there?"

Piper tried to laugh, but it sounded like a nervous thing as if he was wondering whether he made the right choice of returning the ship. "Fuck'n hate storms, but all in a day's work?"

"Seems so."

Piper lifted his free hand towards the rest of the crew. "Don't fret about me. I'll be fine once I dry out."

I spent the rest of the afternoon healing even minor scrapes because I didn't want any type of ill to spread through the crew. Some of them fought my care, but I used the excuse of properly introducing myself as that allowed me to get close enough to stop any bleeding and soothe friction burns from the ropes.

After the long day, I headed back to Captain Hook's cabin. I was finding his space quickly felt more like home than the last, even after all those years. The combination of moonlight and candles made the room soft and almost magical in a way.

On the bed was a pile of blankets. None of the colors coordinated to look like anything besides a hodgepodge of warmth. "How come I've seen this whole ship and still your pile of blankets is what surprises me the most?"

Hook shifted underneath them. "You wouldn't be judging what a man does in the privacy of his own bed, now would you?"

"Nay," I laughed. "I intend to take advantage of that

very thing."

Hook sat up against the headboard, and my eyes couldn't seem to lift from his mismatched pair. "I'll have you know," he started sounding like a fearsome captain, but what followed was far more silly. "My fingers get cold on the best days."

I smiled. "Your circulation must be poor. Give me your hand."

Cautiously, Hook pulled them out from under the blankets and silently waited to see what I did next. My hands were warm on his, but it was the magic that tugged in my chest as his fingers no longer felt bone cold.

"Thank you." It seemed like there were more words on his lips, but I wasn't sure what until his gaze gained a predator's focus. My heart stirred like prey that might prefer to be caught. *What would happen if I continued to be in his path?*

As if to answer, Hook's fingers brushed under my chin, and I leaned in to find his kiss. There were quick teasing brushes of his lips that left me hungry for more. Even as my lips parted to gasp, his tongue only traced my lower lip. I barely held back a whine as he stopped.

"What in this wild wondrous world do you want, darling?" His mouth moved to my neck, leaving a trail of hot kisses.

It felt cruel to try to make me think about desires other than him right now. "I want everything."

Hook growled a pleasing sound that made me feel like nothing mattered outside of his room, outside of the here and now. "Lie back. I want to see if you taste like the sea."

I obeyed without thinking before my thoughts caught back up to me. "I don't think that makes sense."

"Stop being such an intellectual."

His words were a lighthouse that led me away from danger, and I grinned like a fool as I undid the laces of my pants.

"I'm going to drive every thought out of that pretty little head of yours."

"Nothing but you in there." I stared up at the wood-paneled ceiling and measured my breaths.

"That's a good start," Hook said. He pulled my dick free from my pants, stroking it up and down with hands that felt cool again against the heat of my arousal. "So, you made this for yourself?"

I wasn't in the right frame of mind to follow his thought, so I sat up a bit and got a view of him rubbing his fingers down the length of my cock. The sight alone threatened to push me over the edge, and I fell back on the bed. "Yeah, all me."

"Is everything you do a work of art?" Hook asked, warm breath against the sensitive skin. His mouth continued to move lower, enveloping me in a slickness that caused my back to arch up.

I never thought of myself as a work of art, and I soon didn't care what I was as long as I was *his*.

Hook pulled away on the cusp of me fully losing myself to pleasure. "I need to have more of you."

"Like this?"

Hook didn't signal no before he grabbed the lube from the beside and spread it over his fingers. His muscular and hard body moved to lie down as if to cuddle. "Can I fuck you like this instead?"

Feeling like I needed to be touched more than life itself, I just nodded as he slid an arm over my chest.

Spooning naked had a level of intimacy that I never imagined I would have with him before. My fantasies never involved us being a couple—only feeding any desire quickly. They never drew forth more lust out of me than before I started.

His hand started with a gentle exploration with a finger as he left roaming kisses along my neck. Then, he added another finger to slowly stretch me out, ebbing back and forth like a teasing tide.

Oh. 'You fuck like the ocean.' I knew what he meant now. Effortless. Instinctual. Moving as if true to nature. I could sink to the ocean floor within the depth of this feeling and stay there forever.

Even when he moved back to add more lube, our bodies stayed in sync thanks to the waves rocking the ship. At his first thrust, I turned my head into the pillow to keep from moaning loud enough to wake the crew.

"Don't hold back. I want to hear it," Hook whispered wickedly into my ear. "I want you to be so loud that every musician writes a sonnet about you and the pleasure you find."

"Aye, Captain," I softly teased, and it was the last coherent thought I had before my body seemed to know nothing else but pure pleasure.

He moved within me, and I was no longer even yearning for release, simply happy to ride this feeling for as long as it lasted. I was unaware my body could even make such pleased sounds. Carefully, I pressed my body further back against his tantalizing warm skin and hard muscular edges.

Hook grunted before he found words. "I want to pull out and come along your hip. Think I need to see myself on you to truly believe I'm able to touch a body this beautiful."

Even his dirty talk was loving. "I'm all yours."

My lungs hitched as he pulled out and made quick work of himself. I rolled onto my back, feeling messy and loving every second as ecstasy crashed over me. Hook moved off the bed as I held still, content beyond my wildest dreams. We probably *were* heard, but I hardly cared over how good I felt in a body I had worked so hard to have and protect.

He returned with a wet cloth and quietly began cleaning me up. His satisfied expression made me feel proud about it all. Another soft whine escaped me as he brushed over my spent cock.

"There. Good as new," Hook said as he tossed the cloth away.

"Better than new." I reached out for his hand, catching his hook and tugging on the prosthetic so he would come back to bed.

"Are you always this sentimental about sex?" Hook asked and sat back down on the bed.

"No, but it's more than that." I sat up, cupping his face and guiding his gaze to me. "I don't know why I fought my feelings for you for so long."

"If there's one thing I learned out here, it's that things happen when the time is right." He kissed my forehead before taking a second to just look at me and smile. "I love you, darling."

"I love you, Captain."

His eyes darkened like he wanted a round two. "How do you ever decide which to call me?"

I pulled one of his plush blankets over my shoulders. "It's a feeling mostly. Sometimes I pick which I think you'll get a kick out of. I try not to ever shout your name out since it's a secret I like to hold close to my heart."

He let out a delighted growl as he kissed me. "Exactly where I like to be."

"Forever."

"Promises, promises," he added with a small nip at my mouth.

"Aye." It was an agreement, and so much more. "I think I'm going to love my life here."

"We are lucky to have you. *I'm* lucky to have you." Hook kissed me again before he pulled away and got dressed. "Now it's my turn to go see to the crew. I pray no one else gets hurt so you can have a day off."

"Don't spoil me too much."

"Only as much as you deserve."

We might have a difference of opinion there, but I adored that he might have lavished me in gold if I had wanted it. But having a calm day and being needed only in an emergency was nice too. My everything, actually. "Maybe I'll paint today."

He leaned in for another kiss before pulling back. "I must go for a bit before the sight of you leaves me too hungry to ever leave this room."

"See you again soon." It was one of the simplest and best truths I ever allowed myself.

CHAPTER FOURTEEN
— WARREN —

The wind blew through the short ends of my hair. Wind was filled with the scent of salt and freedom. The ship softly rocked along with a swell as I watched Smee, Mack, and another member of the crew buzz around the deck. Their steps were apart yet attuned to each other. One coiled up unused rope, another lit an oil lamp, and the last started climbing up to the lookout.

"Beautiful night, ain't it?" Hook asked before his arms wrapped around me.

I leaned back into him, holding onto the calm for as long as we were granted it. "Piper chose this path?"

"Aye, we're headed towards another coastal town." His mouth hovered near my ear, voice dropping to a near whisper. "Can't fancy why I'd venture on land given what an excellent bed warmer you are."

I chuckled and kept my eyes on the horizon. "Is that what I am?"

Hook purred an agreement in my ear before he started kissing down my neck. I might've believed the clear lie for a second if he wasn't being so soft and deliberate. "And so much more."

"Damn right," I teased back and turned in his arm to face him.

His hand reached up to brush a short strand of hair out of my face that used to be a part of my braid. His fingers lingered along my cheek and then my lips before he seemed to catch himself. "You cut your hair?"

A follow up question was clear in his tone, and I nodded and took a moment. The wind messed up his correction already, but he didn't seem to care. "Every time I make a big life changing choice for myself, I cut it all. Then, I leave just that piece growing until the next. The length helps remind me of how far I've come."

Hook smiled and leaned in to kiss my forehead. The movement caused the golden ring in his ear to glint in the low lantern light. "What else are you thinking?"

"The castle's books told of superstitions that claimed gold earrings could save sailors from drowning. Other passages mentioned the rings could heal illness," I said, a bit unfocused until I held his gaze. "I was wondering if those tales were about being loved by someone, or propaganda to mark you as a pirate easier."

"Does it matter?"

"I don't care if you were deemed villainous," I said with a shake of my head. "Who are our enemies out here?"

Hook glanced up to Mack standing in the crow's nest. "The Queen's men who didn't run from her legacy even after her death. Some have gone rogue now—bloody mercenaries in it for profit."

What I hadn't expected was running into an enemy ship before we made land again. Hook stood at the helm, voice booming over afternoon rain. "Give no quarter!"

Everyone had grown still to look out at the Cards' sails before breaking out of their stupor at the sound of his voice. The crew on deck doubled their usual speed in order to bring the ship around so the cannons were facing the enemy ship as others packed the gunpowder.

The thunderous charges went off in a sequence that was off by a beat. I think the crew was... afraid. Cautious, at very least. And I couldn't blame them because I had never seen a sail like this one before. None of the Queen's guards had ever worn a club. They were nightmare-fuel her court used to threaten obedience in mage children. *"You think she's harsh? Just wait until you see real violence..."*

Their ship was fast and moved near enough that, after the first round of charges, more threatened to harm both ships if fired at such close range.

"Piper!" I yelled at the top of my lungs and spun around to look for him. He definitely wasn't standing on any of the decks, and I was about to search for him below until I found him crouching down beside the stairs. "Stop being a chicken and start playing!"

He quickly glanced towards me as I spoke before looking back at the enemy ship. "It's storming, and I'm not a fighter."

I glanced over my shoulder to the two crews that looked almost near enough to draw their swords on each other. "It's literally your job to help!"

"I hate this job!" Piper yelled back, hand on the railing as he pulled himself up to stand.

"If you break a single fingernail, I'll fix it."

"Yeah?" he said, clutching the pipe tighter between his two hands. "What will you do for my waterlogged soul?"

Hook glided across the deck on a rope. Knocking the first of their boarding party into the water, before dropping down and drawing his sword. "To arms!"

"*Now*, Piper!" I commanded, and he flinched, starting to play with a cuss-filled grumble I couldn't make over the clash of swords. The familiarity of his song buffed the crew—making them brave and connected to each other despite any worry that remained while distracting the invaders.

One of the crew climbed up the ratline, leaving the Card that had been swinging for him without a target. Now, the enemy moved up the quarterdeck towards us. Piper didn't even see him yet, so I decided to test Hook's theory that I could use magic to literally fight back.

With a thought, the attacker's blood pressure dipped low, and the Card dropped to the deck just as Piper turned to see him. Piper gasped and stopped playing in surprise. His wide eyes found mine as he gestured down to the man he must've assumed was dead.

"Vasovagal syncope," I explained to the clueless musician before crouching to bind his attacker's hands. "He's just passed out."

Piper forced a smile before stepping closer to me to play some more. The song wasn't responsible for the day's victory, but it definitely made things easier on the lot of us. By the end, the storm had injured more people. The Card's senseless anger made them no real match for a crew that was willing to fight for themselves and each other.

It felt unreal to watch the surviving Cards marched off the plank as their ship sank in the background. I was left amazed that my greatest fears had all come true, and yet I felt better than ever. With a hope that felt bountiful for once, I turned towards the crew to see who had wounds that needed tending. As I made my rounds healing anything from cuts to bruises, Piper continued playing. His melodies guided the ship, filling the sails with fair winds towards a calm sea.

I wondered if I should volunteer to watch for land until the Captain gave me an order and reminded me exactly where I belonged. "Come here."

Effortlessly, I was pulled close and slipped my hand into his, finding a reassuring squeeze that reminded me that adventure awaited ahead. But, as I breathed in the open ocean air, I believed it was a future that we could handle happily together.

"O Captain, my Captain," I said with a grin. "The ship has weather'd every rack, but what prize is won?"

"Oh darling heart," Hook ad-libbed, making something new and wondrous. "It's here on the deck where my love lives."

"Aye, that's exactly what we'll do," I said, nodding at the very idea of *life*. Us and a crew only known to each other. "The seas will be a dangerously safe and opaque place with us on it. No need to be seen or understood by those on land."

Hook laughed, nipping at my mouth. "Stop sweet talking me."

Discover More Big Bad Deeds In:

PERILOUS PIED PIPER

A sleepy coastal town just signed on a perilously magical new hire that reveals the mayor's heart and stunning empty pocketbook.

The Mayor of Hamelin

Everyone fears rats, so I never expected someone to claim the bounty. Then Piper struts into town all color and song and fixes the problem in a single afternoon. When I can't pay, his playful banter turns into outright extortion. Threatening my reelection with a series of escalating pranks that I refuse to admit are actually funny.

The Pied Piper

I know Mayor Finch of Hamelin respects the law, so I can cash out if I push him. If he can't afford me, a scandal is definitely too high of a price. Pushing his buttons and watching him squirm is far more fun anyway. I'd call it foreplay, but election season is so drawn out it might count as my longest relationship.

Playing dirty keeps me untouchable but drawing this heated tension out further might tie me up in endless red tape. Despite the delight I take in tormenting him, I find myself wanting him to win. In the end, will I be one left with a broken heart?

Perilous Pied Piper is a standalone gay fantasy romance featuring an enemies to lovers retelling with sex, magic, and money with a guaranteed a happily ever after!

ABOUT THE AUTHOR

Rose Sinclair is the profane community leader who started with a blog in 2013. The biggest noise maker they spearheaded was a protest in 2015 that made GLADD step up for the wider LGBTQIA+ community, paving the way for future acceptance for people and on-screen TV representation. Before becoming a full-time writer, they popularized several terms, and set up a decentralized support system with a "Dear Abby" style approach. They are the author of HELLO WORLD, the BIG BAD MAGIC fantasy romance series, and plenty of other queer love stories.

Don't forget to drop your email at
RoseSinclair.com so you don't miss out on
any new releases and get exclusive free stories!